THE

NIECE

BOOK FOUR OF THE MAGICAL WAYS SERIES

YASMINA KOHL

Yasmina Kehl

Yasmina Kohl

Published by ICB Publishing

Copyright 2012

Edited By Betty Iversen

Other books by Yasmina Kohl

Magical Ways Series

Cassandra's Heart [Book 1]

Saver's Savior [Book 2]

A Swindler's Redemption [Book 3]

DEDICATION

There has been an unsung hero for me these last few months, Gessica. And yes that is spelled right. She is the one who takes plain ol' me and turns me in to Yasmina for all of my events. She is awesome and rocks. And if you ever end up in our tiny little town make sure to stop by the Spa and tell her. Oh and just so you know her boss is Kat, is just as awesome. :D

And as usual the family:

My world is only right if you are near me, AC.

Chris, my world will always be slightly off because you aren't in the house any more. For so long you it was just you and me. Make sure that The Army take care of you while you're in their house.

Nikki you are a beautiful young woman, remember we all love you.

To the rest of the cast and crew of my life, yep I am a busy little bee. And there is more to come…

CHAPTER ONE

Nickolas Todd was glad when he had finally made it through the queue and the bouncer let him in, though it was obvious he didn't belong there. The music was loud and awful but he seemed to be the only one here to think so.

Nick wandered through the crowd, trying desperately to look at every face. Samantha may play with her hair and clothes but she couldn't change her face...well not with her funds, she couldn't. *'God I need to find her before someone else does.'*

The bar was set up above the dance floor and wrapped around the outer walls of the club, with a half dozen flights of spiral staircases. After having walked the bar floor, Nick worked his way to the closest set of stairs. He shook his head; these guys sure knew how to keep up a theme. The only colors he'd seen were black, white, grey and varying shades of red. He thought he saw a blue drink once.

Still trying to see every face he passed, Nick tapped a few people on the shoulder to get them to turn, but then he would hold his hands up in apology when it wasn't his sister. There was no use trying to talk, he knew they wouldn't hear him, and it was only partially because of the music.

When he first started looking, he had tried to blend in but gave it up after the second night as a bad idea; him trying to blend in here was worse than standing out.

After a half hour he was getting a very familiar feeling, the feeling of defeat, despair, and depression. He wandered into the bathroom to splash some water on his face. He was tired - nearing exhaustion if he was honest with himself.

He wandered back into the fray, walking back up toward the bar area, he leaned against a the railing looking into the mass of rebellion. *'Yeah what a great rebellion, they all look the fucking same.'* He stiffened suddenly when he felt a hand slide across his ass. He spun around and found a kid who did not look old enough to be here standing in front of him.

"Hey," the mop of hair said.

"Yeah?"

"Just wondering what you'd be up for?"

"Nothing with you, I prefer not being in jail."

The mop of hair laughed. Nick thought he had gotten better at telling the sex of the people in these clubs but by the laugh, he knew he was off, again. The boy though, he was funny.

"Oh man, thanks, I needed that."

"Pardon?"

"You thought I was jailbait...god don't I wish. No honey, I pay a lot to look this young."

"Sure ya do kid."

The boy-man laughed again, "You're good for the ego, wish I could keep you around."

"Right, look I've got to go," Nick made a move to pass the boy but found solid muscle instead of the soft frame he was expecting.

"Just so you don't go calling the cops and breaking up a good night, I'm 36 and the fact that you thought I'm under 21 makes an old dog feel real good. Hope you find whatever you're looking for." The boy-man walked off towards the bar getting a drink handed to him before he even spoke.

Nick shook his head, these Goth clubs could really drive a man to drink.

With one last look around, Nick saw color in the sea of black, and he did a double take. There in the sea of black was a single bright day-glow pink head swaying in time with music. The sight, however strange in the club, made him laugh. "There is a real rebel."

***

"Detective, why aren't you at least trying to find my sister?"

"Mr. Todd, your sister is just held up somewhere with her pimp, we don't have time to track down every pimp and ask if they've got some junkie in their stables, not that they would answer anyways."

Nick counted to five before answering, "Detective, my sister may be a user but she has never been a junkie and while she is a prostitute she hasn't had a pimp since she was nineteen. The guy damn near beat her to death because she was too sick with the flu to see her customers."

"Mr. Todd, we'll call you if we find her. Now please, I have cases I need to be working on."

"Bastard," Nickolas Todd muttered to himself unlocking his car. He was bone tired. His sister had been missing almost three weeks now. The cops wouldn't do anything because of what Sam was. He dropped his head onto the roof of his car. He had learned how to translate cop…'we'll call when we find your sister' meant the coroner would call when they had identified her remains on his table.

"Damn it, Sam, where in the hell are you?"

***

Another day, another bar, still no Sam; Nick had lost hope but he had to keep trying. He didn't even have a good picture to show around; she hadn't let him take her picture in years. All he had was a grainy picture of her asleep he had snapped on his cell.

He was beginning to hate the color black, it was all he saw every night. Looking over the small floor in front of him there was black and white again...no Sam.

Just before, from across the bar, he left he saw the boy-man he had seen a week ago. The boy-man raised his eyebrow and tipped his head to the side as if to ask if Nick had found what he had lost. Nick shook his head once, the man bowed his head, and Nick left. He had one more bar to try tonight before he started the whole circuit all over again.

***

At the new bar the music was still awful but at least this group could sing fairly well and it made everything tolerable. It was still too loud, he chuckled to himself. "If it's too loud, your too old," he muttered. He could just make out the words, so that made him feel a little better. Looking over the crowd again, he was looking at the faces hoping, but knowing it was useless.

He had to find Sam, he couldn't handle finding her on a cold metal table, he couldn't go through that again...he never wanted to see the viewing room ever again.

He was the oldest at seventeen and when their parents had been killed in a car crash it was decided he was old enough to identify them.

Sam had only been fifteen at the time but within the year she had started using drugs, and by the time she was seventeen she was turning tricks to pay for her drugs. Then there was the fiasco with Marco. It got her to a hospital and rehab, but it hadn't taken. In all the years she had been torturing herself, she had always let Nick know she was alive, she called at least every three days if she didn't make it home, she had never gone over 72 hours. Tomorrow would be 30 days.

A flash of orange pulled him out of his fugue state. Like the pink weeks before, it was a bright day-glow orange. He shook his head, at least someone was an individual. He decided to make one more round, go home to his empty house, and hope to sleep.

Wandering, he found himself drawn to the orange hair, he knew it wouldn't be Sam. The color would draw too much attention to her and she would never do that. Still he found himself wandering toward the hair, "Hey," He yelled when he got to the orange hair.

"Hey back."

He thought he heard but a flash of red caught his attention for a moment. He shook his head to clear it and then asked, "Do ah, do you know Janie?" Nick asked using the name Sam used when she was working.

"What does she look like?

"Black straight hair, pale face, black eye shadow, red lips and not much on."

"That helps," Orange hair said swaying to the music.

"Yeah, I know."

"Sorry, I can't help."

"That's okay, no one can," Nick left feeling more shattered than ever.

Why had one conversation broken him more than the weeks of looking? Nick made it home but barely. He climbed into his bed and for the first time in seventeen years, he cried himself to sleep.

CHAPTER TWO

"Detective, why do I keep having to say the same thing to you? Do you need a disability discharge for not being able to hear?" Nick was yelling. The entire squad room could hear him and he didn't care. Five weeks and these asses hadn't helped him one bit.

"Mr. Todd."

"Don't Mr. Todd me, you judgmental lazy bastard. You think since my sister has problems she's not worth your time but you're paid to help everyone, even the ones you don't like and think aren't worth it."

"Mr. Todd, sit down," Detective Ford said angrily.

"No, fuck you," Nickolas spun on his heel, slammed the door to the hall open, and managed to walk right into the boy-man he'd seen a few times in the clubs.

"Uh..." dumbfounded Nick couldn't speak.

"Yes, I look very different here don't I?" The man was dressed in a suit, tie, and carried a briefcase.

"Lawyer?"

"Yeah."

"Sue that ass just inside the door for incompetence and laziness, would ya?" Nick said walking through the outer door.

**

Trying yet again, Nick walked into the first bar where he'd seen the lawyer. Nick wasn't looking for the man per say, but he wouldn't not look for him either. Nick did find lime green curls though, he wondered for a second if the green hair was the same as the pink hair he'd seen here the first time.

He stood there for five minutes and each time he caught his gaze sliding over to the green, he'd curse and pull it away looking at faces. The sixth time he saw green he said, "Fuck," and went to the stairs making his way to green hair again.

"Hey," he yelled in a déjà vu moment.

"Hey back," He thought he heard once more...when he found Sam he was going to have to get his hearing checked.

"You seen Janie?"

"What's she look like?"

"Same as last time."

"Still not helpful."

"I still know."

"You want," the yelling stopped as the music changed from screaming to a softer ballad song, still too loud but you could almost not yell, "You want to go have coffee?"

"Huh?"

"You've been looking for Janie for at least a week, you look tired and strained. How about coffee, quiet, and an ear?"

"Uh, sure."

"There's a shop two blocks over."

"Ok, I'll follow you."

Green hair walked up the spiral stairs case ahead of him, waving at a few people as she went. Nick shook his head as he realized that her ass was inches from his face as they went up the stairs and he didn't even care.

CHAPTER THREE

They dropped in chairs of the all night coffee shop drinking their gift from the gods in silence.

"How do you walk in those things?" Nick asked pointing at her shoes.

"Lots of practice," Green hair said lifting her five-inch patent leather boots off the floor, "I'm Melissa by the way."

"Nickolas."

"So who is Janie?"

"She's my sister, uh...Samantha actually. She uses Janie when she goes out."

"Why are you looking for her?"

"She..."

Melissa watched him struggle with memories that seemed to hurt. "She hasn't been home for over a month."

"Okay."

"She has never, in sixteen years, been gone more than 72 hours without calling or showing up."

"Okay, cops?"

"Are assholes and need to be beaten."

"A sore spot."

"Samantha has had problems."

"Hmmm."

"She uses and she..."

"I get it."

"They don't think she's worth looking for, he keeps saying she's with a pimp somewhere."

"No?"

"NO! She hasn't had one in fifteen years. She wouldn't go back."

"'K. Private eye?"

"Don't have the money. I..." he stopped when Melissa took out her phone and pressed one button.

He watched her play with the beaded tassels on the red paisley scarf she was wearing. "Emiko, sorry it's so late, you...ok good. Is the love of your...thanks, doll.

Man, sorry to.. no, hey, can you help a guy out? Nope sorry, no, sis, yeah month or more, sure, 10 thanks, later Saver."

Nick's head hurt from the broken conversation, he had tried to follow, but at the end, "Huh," was all he could manage.

Melissa smiled softly and answered his question, "It just so happens, I know a private detective who is starting out, but is flush enough to be able to take pro-bono work."

"If he's starting out, how will he know what to do?"

"Honey, he's starting out as a private eye, not looking for people. He just used to do it on a more... hmm, damn, let's say, if he told me he would have to kill me kind of level, this is child's play for him. A 'retired can't tell' guy," she offered as an explanation.

"Ah, ok," All of this almost made sense to Nick, almost.

"He will find Samantha. Do you have any pictures, even an older one?"

"One from when we were kids. It really doesn't look like her at all anymore. And a grainy cell phone picture."

"Maybe Cassandra could draw her?"

"Like a sketch? The police tried, it didn't look like her."

"Cassandra is talented with more than the pencil, she's off tomorrow. I'll ask her to head over to Saver's tomorrow and see what she can do."

"Saver?"

"It's his nickname; we use it to remind him of how we see him. It's really Xavier St. Cloud."

"Why?" Nick couldn't believe suddenly he had someone who wasn't judging his sister and who knew people who could help.

"Why what?"

"Why are you pulling in favors for me, a free private dick and sketch artist?"

"Um, don't call Saver a private dick, it makes him angry, and you don't want to see him angry. Truuuuust me, you don't; it's a very bad place for him."

"Uh, sure."

"And I'm not calling in favors, I am asking family for help."

"He's your brother?"

"Sort of, I meant family by choice, not birth, most of us are orphans. He's my brother because he's with my sister, Emiko. Who is my sister because she works with me, as are Cassandra, Anne, and well Yvette is more like the mom than sister, but she's not that much older, so we will go with sister, who had to take care of us 'cause mom and dad are gone. My other brothers are James and Robert. We look out for each other and help. If I ask, they will help because they want to. As for your problem with the cops, tell Saver. He'll call Sam, and whoever is an ass will soon be finding out that it's not a good idea."

"Who's Sam?"

"Sam is a buddy of Savers, known him for, well since they started calling him Saver, works for the local LEOs, and is a damn fine guy even for a cop."

Mellissa's phone rang the Godfather theme song; she picked it up. Making a face, she hit what turned out to be ignore, because it stopped ringing immediately.

"Shouldn't you get that?"

"Nope, never do."

"You gave them a ringtone."

"Yep, so I know not to answer it. Not sure how he got the number and I wish he would stop using it."

"Change it." Nick said wondering why she wouldn't have thought of that.

"No man, the number is perfect, not giving it up."

"A perfect number?"

"Yep 696-9690."

"How is it perfect?" Nick paused as he thought of the numbers she had said and realized that it would be easy to remember, and for those with sick imaginations it would be a good visual. "Ok you got me, it's perfect."

"Yep 'cause the last guy is so flexible that he doesn't need a partner."

Nick had just taken a drink of his coffee and ended up choking on the fine brew.

"Sorry, should have warned you my sense of humor is as off color as my hair."

Drawing in a breath finally, he replied, "Thanks. About the hair, why?"

"Cause I can and it's not the real one."

"You don't like…"

Nick hadn't even finished the question before she answered, "NO."

Having only been with Melissa about a half-hour Nick was in no way an expert, but it was very obvious that her real hair color was a very sore spot and not something that should ever be mentioned.

The Godfather rang again "Damn him, he won't stop."

"Why does he have the theme to the godfather as …?"

"Because he is."

"Your Godfather?"

"Not anymore," Melissa said only to herself.

Nick was sure that he was going to have to get his hearing checked now because it sounded like to him she had said, "Not anymore," but like the hair, it seemed like a subject not to be broached.

"Look, it's late and I need to head off to bed. I have to be to work at 9 and you need to be at Savers at 10."

"Where is his office?"

"Over on State at the corner of Broadway."

"Isn't that all industrial?" he said in confusion.

"Yeah, most of it is, but Max's wife works over there and has been broken into a lot, so he's there for help. It's only a storefront down. Since he opened, she hasn't had any more problems. I think they realized messing with a witch's shop with a special ops marine one door down was a really dumb ass move."

"Ok." Special ops marine as a private eye who watched out for a witch, what the hell had he gotten himself into?

"Word got around quick."

Raising an eyebrow at the understatement Nick said, "I bet."

"Had some help from Sam but word got around," Melissa said wrapping her cloak around her shoulders and sauntering out of the shop.

CHAPTER FOUR

Nick slept better than he had in weeks, but considering most nights he didn't sleep at all, that was easy to do. As he readied for his meeting with St. Cloud, he wondered what the man was going to be like. Melissa had said he was a special ops marine and flush enough to take on pro-bono work. Nick figured he'd have to be an older man, he just hoped that he would be open minded enough to be able to go where he needed to find Sam, and to be able to ignore why she was lost in the first place. Melissa must have thought it would be okay when she called him.

Pulling up in front of the building, he was sure he was in the right spot. There was an American flag and a Marine Corps flag hanging in each of the windows on either side of the door that read *Save Them for Me*. Nick parked his car in the lot on the side, grabbed the folder off the seat with what precious little he had about Sam, and took a deep breath.

He walked to the door, opened, and stopped short. Sitting at the desk was a younger man reading files; Nick shrugged, and asked, "Is your father here?"

"Father?" the man said looking up, raising an eyebrow.

"I'm looking for Xavier St. Cloud."

When the man stood up, Nick could feel the power and authority the man exuded. He had heard people say things like that, how they could feel someone's strength, but until now he had thought they were exaggerating.

"Guessing Melissa didn't tell you too much about me?"

Chuckling nervously Nick replied, "Not nearly enough."

Xavier held out his hand to Nick and introduced himself, "Xavier St. Cloud, known as Saver to most around here."

"Nickolas Todd and I answer to Nickolas or Nick," Nick was not a small man, six foot even, hundred eighty pounds, so he was a good size, but he felt tiny compared to Xavier. As he was about to ask another question he felt something ripple around him, he shivered and then the door opened.

"Cassandra, dial it down, you're giving Nick the shivers."

"Huh, what, oh crap, sorry had a very good morning."

Saver shivered and said, "Uh huh, I'm still getting used to your good morning, so back it off, would ya?"

Nick turned to see a gorgeous brunette standing in the doorway, and he had no other way to explain it but to say she was glowing. She closed her eyes and took a few deep breaths and the glow shimmered and disappeared.

"Thank you, the last time you came in here after a 'good morning' you damn near fried my computer."

"I did not, Saver, stop exaggerating."

"Ha, that will be the day," said a man opening the door behind the brunette that obviously was Cassandra.

"Sam, don't you have a donut to go eat? Geez, old man, you gonna let the local donut hole shut down?" Xavier said to the man behind Cassandra.

"I can take you any day of the week, whipper snapper. You just keep it up and I'll have that pretty little girl of yours dose your food," Sam said failing to keep the smile off his face, "she likes me."

Xavier also couldn't keep from smiling but the smile was much smaller compared to the cop's. "Ha, she loves me too much."

"Damn it, foiled again." Sam joked rubbing his hands together like a cartoon villain.

Nick felt like a ping-pong ball, his head bouncing back and forth, between what he hoped was friendly banter. After the trio stopped, Xavier turned toward Nick and introduced him.

"Guys, this is Nick. Melissa called about him last night."

"Yeah, she said to bring paper, and pencil and power."

"Ah well, just keep the last away from my hard drive please." Xavier pleaded.

Sam nodded in Nick's direction and said, "Little shit called and said to bring badge, pen and paper to write names on cause I have no memory left."

"Well you don't, geezer. Nick, take a seat. I'm guessing you need all of us if Mel called."

"Gods, Saver, you know she hates that." Cassandra said.

"I know but she's not here to hear it, so I am safe. Why don't you tell us about your sister, Nick?"

Nick sat dazed for a moment; he hadn't had anyone show any interest in his sister in six weeks. Now there were three people sitting waiting for him to spill his guts. He took a deep breath and started, "Samantha is a drug user and a prostitute. If that's a problem then I'll go now and save all your time."

"No problem, she's still your sister," Cassandra said with compassion.

"I don't have a problem," Sam said.

Xavier shrugged his shoulders and said "So."

"It's been a problem at missing persons; Detective Ford won't help and won't let the case be reassigned."

"That won't be a problem anymore, I'll have a chat with him, and I'll make sure I get the case."

"You're in missing persons?"

"No, but I know the captain and have enough pull to get just about any case I want."

"Oh, okay, thank you."

"Nick how long has she been missing?" Cassandra asked softly as if to lighten the burden.

Nick's chest tightened as he answered, "Six weeks, three days and a handful of hours. She's been working the streets since she was seventeen, our parents died when she was fifteen.

I tried to keep her safe but I, I could... couldn't. She started using drugs at sixteen. She was always such a good kid growing up but when our parents were killed in a car accident she couldn't cope, I couldn't get to her to..."

Cassandra stood and walked to Nick who was trying not to cry in front of everyone. "Oh sweetie, it's okay, we understand, you were young. You did what you could, you're looking for your sister; you've never given up on her. Your parents would understand."

Nick could feel himself calming down and Cassandra pulled him into a hug, as he closed his eyes for a moment, he thought the glow had come back but when he opened them again everything looked normal plus he didn't feel the need to find the closest Kleenex box. "Samantha...she.. the cop, he keeps saying she's just with her pimp. But a couple years after she started working the streets, she hooked up with Marco, and he made her work rain or shine, she got the flu and couldn't work. He almost beat her to death because of it. After that she ended up in the hospital. She said she would never have another pimp and in the sixteen years since, she hasn't."

Sam said angrily "Really going to have to have a talk with Ford."

"I'll join you," Xavier said gruffly.

"Think I could sit in on that discussion, boys?" Cassandra said with a very scary look on her face.

"Cass, we want him to be frightened, not scared shitless."

"Aww, I'll play nice," the lady whined.

"No," both men said at the same time.

"Rats, you're no fun."

"That's what you have James for," Xavier joked.

"Not that kind of fun," She said almost pouting.

"Uhhh, guys?" Nick interrupted.

"Sorry, scaring the normal again," Cassandra said, shifting her attention back to the sad, dark haired man.

"Hey, what are we?" Sam questioned

"Family."

"Ah," Xavier said with a shoulder shrug.

"Nick, what else can you tell us?"

"In seventeen years she has never gone more than 72 hours without calling me or showing up at the apartment. She usually sticks to the Goth scene and she goes by Janie when she's working. I have some pictures but they're old. She hasn't let me take a picture of her in years. A year ago I snuck one on my cell phone but its grainy and dark because she was asleep."

"She ever get arrested?" Sam asked.

"No, somehow she manages to steer clear of the vice squad, both for the drugs and the tricks. Melissa said..."

"I'm working on it," Cassandra said, her pencil already to paper.

"I haven't shown you..."

"Don't need it," Cassandra said waving her hand toward the file.

'*These people are crazy*,' Nick shook his head "I've been to every club in town multiple times trying to find her, I can't. Hell, a few of the bouncers are letting me in for free because they've seen me so many times."

"Who have you talked to?"

"No one really," Nick shrugged, "they won't talk to me, I'm not part of the society, so they don't really see me."

"I'll take Melissa with me, she knows these people, she can help. Wish I had

Sh..." Xavier stopped and absently rubbed his shoulder.

Sam said, "I know, Saver, I know," the two men paused with a strange look between them but Nick couldn't decipher it.

"Saver," Cassandra said softly

"I know, I'm not going there."

"Yes you were."

"Damn woman, you're irritating," Xavier grumbled.

"Yep, but I grow on you."

Shivering but looking up Xavier said with a light chuckle, "Like a freaking mold. You're as bad as Emiko. Least you don't sing."

"Don't know the words."

"How long have you guys known each other?" Nick asked, totally lost between the dynamic of the trio.

Sam answered first, "I've known Xavier since he was about six days old. Xavier and I have only known Cassandra a few months, he's engaged to..."

"Emiko." Nick said remembering what Melissa had said the night before.

"Yeah." Xavier said.

"The whole family by choice thing?" Nick asked

"Something like that." Sam said.

"So what, you're the uncle?" Nick asked the cop.

"Suppose so."

Cassandra stood again and handed him a sheet of paper. When Nick took it he got the chills, the face looking back at him was very near to what his sister looked like. "How...I...how?" he couldn't form the question.

"You're brother and sister, your bone structure would be similar. Besides you're shouting her picture to me."

"What?"

"Cassandra," Xavier said with little patience in his voice.

"Well he is."

"I am what?"

Sam chuckled and answered, "Cassandra here, is a well, a witch."

"I thought Crystal was the witch?" Nick asked seriously confused.

"I wish I had half the abilities our Cassandra has," A woman said walking through the curtain in the back.

"I don't have power, I just am," Cassandra said matter-of-factly.

"You just are, my butt." Crystal retorted, "Lunch, Xavier," She set a tray down and walked back out.

"This is how she pays me Sam, with rabbit food." Xavier curled his lip up at the lunch but started to eat it anyway.

Sam just laughed, "You knew you weren't gonna get any steak out of this arrangement."

"I know," chuckling, he ate the large salad, "Max got to it though, there's bacon chunks in it. About your sister, any scars, or tattoos?"

"One scar, on her left knee about an inch long."

"Eyes, hair color, height..."

"Brown eyes, black hair, about 5'6. Her weight changes too much depending on whether or not she's..." Nick said trailing off again.

Sam tried to let the man know his pain was understood, "It's okay, we get it Nick. I've got to ask, what's her..."

"Heroin."

"Okay, that helps narrow down the leg work a bit. Don't suppose you know her dealer of choice do you?"

"Used to be Leister 'till he got sent up."

"I can find out who took over his clients," Sam offered.

"Thanks Sam."

"I'll head over and talk to the Captain about Ford and Leister. Give me a call when you get her sketch done, Cassandra."

" 'K, shouldn't be too much longer, just a few tweaks."

Sam nodded and left.

Xavier stood behind his chair and then wandered the small office. "Why didn't you go to someone before?"

"I handle tech support for an online company, I don't make that much money, I couldn't afford to go to anyone and I mistakenly thought that the police would help."

"Oh, they will once Sam gets done with Ford. He'll wish he never joined the force." Xavier explained.

"I thought you were going to go too."

"Oh, I'll have a talk with Ford on my own."

"Why do I suddenly feel bad for Ford?"

"Don't worry about him," came another voice from behind. Nick turned to find Melissa standing in the door.

"Thought you were working today?" Cassandra asked.

"Was, but it was slow, so Yvette said to take the rest of the day."

"Don't you have something you would rather be doing?" Nick wondered.

"Don't want me around? I can take a hint," Melissa said turning to leave.

"No, no, that's not what I said. I just don't know why you would want to come here instead of..." The look from Melissa made Nick stop without finishing his thought.

"Don't have much to do during the day."

"Melissa, I was hoping you would be able to go with me to talk to people at a few of these clubs. Get them to look at the sketch. Nick mentioned how no one would talk to him."

"No, they wouldn't really. I can try and get them to talk to you, but I doubt it will work."

"Got to start somewhere and until we find out who took over Leister's turf, it's the only place."

"Well, this is it," Cassandra said handing the final sketch to Nickolas.

"She doesn't have a scar on her chin though," He said, wondering why she would add such a mark when he told her she only had a scar on her knee.

"Sorry Nick, but I think she does now," Cassandra replied with sadness in her voice.

"How would you... I don't understand," Nick sighed.

Cassandra shrugged, "Me neither sometimes, but that's what she looks like."

Nick looked at the sketch, with the exception of the scar it was right on. The first copy she had shown him was very close but it had been a little bit off, the nose a little too short, her eyes a little too shallow but this one, this sketch was Samantha exactly.

"I hadn't realized how old she looked," he slouched back in his chair, his sister was only 32 but she looked almost 50 in the sketch.

"Nick, let me take you to get something to eat and then maybe you should try to get some rest," Melissa offered.

"I have to start my shift soon," Nick said shaking his head.

"If this wasn't a good time you could have said something," Melissa felt like she had somehow steamrolled over Nick.

"No, it's fine, I just, I need some time to…" Nick stood, "I've got to go," he said leaving the office quickly.

"Why do I have that effect on men?" Melissa asked quietly, momentarily forgetting who she was with.

Cassandra answered her back, "Because you speak your mind and it scares them sometimes."

Xavier nodded in agreement "Well, the hair's kinda out there too, kid."

Melissa rounded on Xavier, "Kid?"

"You're younger than me, that makes you kid."

"So what's Emiko? She's younger than me."

"By a few days," Xavier qualified, "and she's my little one."

Cassandra spoke up "Uh, guys, did anyone get Nick's number or address?"

"Well shit," Xavier said, "Call Sam, he can look him up. No wait, his info should be in Samantha's case file, so won't need to."

"Yep, all right. I'll call and ask while I'm getting the fax number to send the sketch."

"I'm gonna head home since I'm not going to lunch," Melissa said, "Give me a call when you want to head out, Saver."

"Will do."

CHAPTER FIVE

At Melissa's little house, she sat on the stool next to the door and unlaced her boots. She really wished that Nick had taken her up on the offer for lunch. She had nothing to do and she was hungry but she really hated cooking, but she also hated eating alone.

Setting her boots in the closet next to the rest of her collection, she wandered into the kitchen. Grabbing an apple and a container of caramel sauce, she went to the spare bedroom she had turned into a computer/toy room.

Picking up her favorite knife off the table, she cut the apple into strips while her computer loaded up one of her forum sites. Sighing, she popped an apple chunk in her mouth before the copious amount of caramel dripped off.

Checking to see how many emails she had at the forum, she sighed again. Looking at each tag line, she hit delete without even reading them. Everyone started one of two ways; let me dominate you or I'll let you dominate me.

"I just want a little fun, not a life thing," she finally said out load.

Her phone rang and it took all of her self-control not to throw it across the room as the Godfather theme began to play. "I really need to change my number, but why should I? Damn it, he said he was out of my life and he would answer if I called, not that he would call."

The phone stopped playing the instrumental song and Melissa sighed for a third time. Looking at the site, Melissa shook her head. Instead, she decided to do a quick Google image search for bondage. That came up with a few nice pictures but nothing worthwhile. "Maybe I'll hit the other clubs when Saver's done tonight," she said aloud.

Melissa had always talked aloud to herself. Over the years, it had bothered more than one partner that she could and would have whole conversations by herself.

Deciding the internet was not going to hold her interest today, Melissa went to her bathroom and drew a bath. The house she lived in was just right for one person. When she moved to the small city, she decided she would use some of the 'seed money' from Aniello to put a down payment on it. She worked hard every month to make the mortgage payment and take care of her little haven.

Melissa added a generous helping of Pomegranate bubble bath, then picked up the book from the nightstand beside her bed. It had been a gift from a friend and she just couldn't get into it. Her friend had meant well when she gave it to Melissa but it was just not her cup of tea. Deciding against the book, she dropped it back onto the stand where it had sat for months collecting dust.

Sinking into her mid-day bath, Melissa dropped her head onto the bath pillow and tried to forget Aniello, Nick, and all those idiots on the forum. The day was turning into a wash, in more than one way.

Melissa pulled on her nipple rings, but felt nothing. "Crap" she said, "This sucks, I want sex and can't find anyone. I'm not that damn fussy, really, boobs or dicks I don't care. Why can't I find someone?" Leaning her green hair back once more to the pillow Melissa said, "Screw you all, I'll just sleep and dream about sex."

Forty-five minutes later Melissa woke from her nap to a chilled bath and her phone ringing again. This time it was the theme song to CHiPs. "Fuck, Sam, I'll never make it to my phone, so you better leave a message." Getting out of the tub she dried off and threw on her robe; it matched perfectly with her hair. Silk was her obsession. She had a silk robe to match every color Mike used on her hair. Her phone rang once more to the Godfather, "Mother fuck Aniello, leave me the hell alone."

Picking up her phone, when she opened it to check for messages from Sam, Bewitched started to play. "Oh for Christ sakes, yes Cassandra." she said exasperated.

"Testy much?"

"Let's see, since I left you, Aniello has called three times, Sam called while I was getting out of the bath tub and now you, so yes, testy much."

"Why don't you call him back?"

Melissa said, "I'll call Sam as soon as I'm done talking to you," purposely ignoring the fact that Cassandra had meant Aniello.

Melissa heard Cassandra sigh; the empath continued on, "I sent the sketch to Sam and he's put it in the missing person database country wide. Samantha's picture will run on the 6:30 news on Channel Four with a little information. Sam doesn't want to mention the things Samantha is into, we all want people to be sympathetic and help Nick."

"Cool, did Saver say what time we're going to meet and head out?"

"No, not yet."

"Tell him to give me a call."

"Will do, are you okay honey?"

"I'm fine mom, stop worrying."

"I can't, you've been down lately and paler than usual."

"I'm fine, I'm just bummed. I'm looking for *my* James and Saver and not finding anyone."

"They are out there, just got to wait your turn."

"I know, and I'm trying to be patient, but hey, it's me, I don't have any."

"Trust Melissa, trust," the click in Melissa's ear told her that Cassandra made sure she got the last word in by hanging up on her.

"Oh well," dialing her voicemail she heard Sam's message that they had found who had taken over Leister's territory and that he and Saver were going to have a 'talk' with the man, and that Saver would call about going tomorrow night instead.

"Great, so I'm free," Melissa said grouchily. "I want something to do. I should have argued with Yvette about leaving early, damn it."

She hadn't argued because she had wanted to spend time with Nick. There was something about his sad eyes, those sad blue grey eyes. His voice was something that had made her listen. It was soft and commanding at the same time. Not like Saver's commanding 'you will do this because if you don't I'll kill you', but a 'you will do this because you want to' tone.

A shiver ran up her back as a thought of Nickolas leaning over her flashed through her mind. "Fuck, I need to get laid." However, the thought of sex just brought the image back; he was naked from the waist up and was twisting her nipple ring. "Fuck, fuck, fuck," Melissa said stomping to her room to put her clothes back on.

CHAPTER SIX

About three hours later she was at a club none of her family knew she frequented. Saver would kill her and Sam would have a coronary for sure. Melissa thought Yvette knew she went to something like MINE!, but neither talked about it.

After showing her membership card, Melissa wandered in looking for someone to catch her attention. Sitting at the bar and signaling for her usual drink, she turned to watch the floor.

'*Damn it, nothing,*' Melissa shook her newly darkened hair. Feeling a tap on her shoulder, she took the Celtic Kiss from the bartender and sipped it.

"Nice color Mel."

Setting her drink down, Melissa turned to face the femmedom. Trying to be polite Melissa replied, "Marishka, nice to see you.

"So when are you going to come to my room, little bit?"

"Hmm, Marishka, you know your room is not my scene, you're a little too heavy for me."

"But you'll learn to love it," Marishka said, breathing heavily into Melissa's ear.

Rolling her eyes, Melissa turned and picked up her drink giving herself an excuse to move from the overly dominating woman who seemed to live at MINE!

Melissa poured on the charm, "Darling, I'm not the good little sub you're looking for. You know this, so why do you keep trying?"

"Because someday you'll realize you are a good little sub."

"No, someday you'll realize I'm no one's sub. I may like it a little rough and don't mind being tied down, but you really hate pushy bottoms so - back off," The last was said with force and a small growl.

"You'll find me someday Mel and you'll like it," Marishka said, leaving the bar for the hall that lead to the rooms.

"One day, one day," Melissa said into her drink. Still looking over the floor, she found someone who sparked her interest. Walking over with her drink, she leaned against the railing that separated the bar area from the dance floor.

"Christophe," Melissa said to the man standing next to her. They had been together off and on for years.

"Melissa dear, what are you doing here?"

"Looking for a little something."

"Well, we both know I'm not little."

"I know dear, but you are just what I want," Melissa said draining the rest of her drink.

"Well, I am meeting someone but not for hours."

"See, now you know why you showed up so early."

"I do indeed," Christoph said holding out his arm for Melissa to take.

Leaving the floor for the hall, Melissa didn't hear the announcer say that Janie would be the next performer.

Entering an empty toy room, Christophe lifted up Melissa and set her on the bed. "We should meet somewhere other than MINE! dear."

"I know, but then this would be something else," she said throwing herself back onto the bed, letting Christophe's hand glide up her leg and under her skirt. When he retraced the path down he pulled on the lace of her boot. Finishing with one, he repeated the same thing with the other leg.

"You have the best shoes, my dear."

"Thank you," Melissa said throatily when Christophe's fingers brushed her pussy.

"Naughty girl, you're not wearing panties," pulling on her clitoris clip.

A gasp escaped her lips, "I know."

"Knew what you were going to get, dear?"

"Yes," she moaned when one finger slid in.

"Take off your skirt," Christophe demanded.

Letting him take the lead today, Melissa did as he ordered, unhooking the belt style closures on the side of her skirt. All the while Christophe was finger fucking her pussy. When his hand dipped lower and he felt the second piece of jewelry dangling from her ass he sucked in his breath, "I know you just got your hair done dear, I can smell Mike's cologne on you."

"Yes, I just left there," she answered truthfully.

"You went to Mike's with no panties, this short skirt and jewelry on you pussy and in your ass. You deserve to see Marishka for that. Roll over," He growled.

Melissa did as she was told and was ecstatic when Christophe left his hand in her pussy; she gasped when she felt his other hand hit her bare ass, but purred when she felt him kiss the reddened handprint. "You are such a bad, bad girl," And a second smack on her other cheek came.

She cried out again and thrust back onto his hand.

"No, no, you will hold still."

'*Damn it*' she thought '*no*'. She had to think to be still.

Feeling him pull his hand from her pussy she whimpered, he had said to be still, not be silent, but she had to bite her lip to keep from jerking when she felt the cold ice replace his fingers.

"That's better, dear."

Christophe and Melissa had a convenient relationship, when they were at MINE! and wanted each other, they would take turns as to who was in control. Last time Christophe had wanted to let go and feel, he hadn't wanted to think. Melissa had taken the roll as Dom and used every toy she could on the man, who looked all of seventeen.

Later he told her that he had wanted to forget the day, he had lost a case, and a man not worth the air he breathes was walking around free.

Thinking about now as she felt the first drops of the melting ice leave her. Making her want to cry out. She was so horny. God, she wanted to be fucked so badly.

"I know you do my dear."

The little midnight haired Goth bit her tongue, not realizing she had spoken aloud.

"I'll get to fucking you soon Melissa, very soon," Christophe said from behind her.

Melissa felt something else slide into her and knew it was one of the glass dildos that the club supplied. This one must have been in a warming drawer because it contrasted with the ice already there.

Panting, Melissa fought the urge to rub her clit on the table. Christophe knew her body and knew what would send her over the edge, but that was the problem. He knew when and where not to touch her, prolonging their time together. When she felt the bed dip next to her, she looked up and saw him next to her.

"You can move but you better not do anything to make yourself come."

Melissa rose over him and almost dove for his cock.

"Oh god, yes," Christophe whispered when she swallowed him.

Bobbing for a few minutes on his thick cock Melissa leaned back and continued the stimulation by jacking him off.

"You are so good at this, but you are so damn good at dominating too, my dear. Oh god," He hissed when she ran a blue fingernail down his chest. "Do you sharpen those by the way?"

'*Two could play at this game*,' she thought. Christophe knew her body but she knew his just as well. "No." she said breathlessly raising up and biting down on his nipple.

"Oh fuck, lie down," he growled.

Doing what he asked, Melissa cried out when he pulled the dildo out and thrust into her.

"You are a pushy bottom," he groaned.

"Sometimes."

Talking no longer became an option due to the pace Christophe set, Melissa raised her bottom up and met him stroke for stroke. Within minutes, they were both shouting they're pleasure.

After a little while Christophe was the first to speak, "As always my dear, superb."

"Thanks to you. Who are you seeing later?"

"Hmmm, this cute aid from the DA's office. Damn if he isn't the sweetest sub."

"Ah, that's why you got all Dom-my on me? Getting in the mood?"

"Hmm, maybe I was," Christophe said, walking to the sink and warming the water.

"That's okay, I don't mind, was your turn anyway."

"True, true, but I could have waited if you were..."

"No, its fine. I didn't care, I just wanted something."

"Obviously no luck in finding the right one."

"No," Melissa sighed, "you would think I'd be better off considering I don't limit myself, but noooo."

"Just got to wait your turn, my dear."

"That's the second time today someone's said that to me."

"It's sage advice."

"Ha, god damn it," Melissa cursed jumping from the bed and hitting ignore on her phone.

Christophe raised a well-manicured eyebrow and let the unasked question hang in the air.

"Don't ask and I won't have to tell."

"Sweetheart, we are not in the military and we both know the other is bi."

"Fine, don't ask and I won't have to lie."

"Melissa, we have been friends and fuck buddies for years, why would you lie to me now?"

"Because of who he is and what he does, and because of who you are and what you do."

"I'm not the DA."

"I know, but still, just leave it, please," Mellissa asked with a hint of fear in her voice.

"Fine," Christophe answered handing her a rag to clean up.

"Thank you."

"So what are you going to do with the rest of the day?"

"Don't know, I'll think of something."

Christopher offered a piece of advice as he kissed Melissa, "Just stay away from Marishka."

"Planned on it."

CHAPTER SEVEN

"Ma'am, you need to calm down and let me explain. Ma'am please," Nick was about ready to pound his head on his desk but that would only make his head ache worse.

"Ma'am. Hey lady!" he yelled. That got her attention. "Thank you, now listen, you need to take the folder that we just put on your desktop and open it, by clicking the mouse twice quickly. Okay, now see the icon that says setup? Click on that. Yes, click install. Now there is a user agreement that you have to read and checkmark the box at the bottom. Yes, you have to agree to the terms or it will not let you install the pro... Ma'am, you have to." Nick said trying hard not to grind his clenched jaw. "Ma'am, if you don't agree to the terms I can't help you any further. Fine Ma'am, when you decide to agree to the terms, call me back and we will go to the next step," Nick threw his head set on the desk and rubbed his neck "Why do they have to be so stupid?" he said to no one. Getting up, the alarm on his desk went off signaling the end of his shift.

"Yes, no one else to piss me off."

Nickolas walked to the kitchen and got an apple and cut it up, found his last caramel dipping sauce and cursed.

"Back to McDonald's."

Wandering around his cramped apartment, Nick tried to work out the kinks in his legs and back from sitting for six hours straight. Taking call center calls is alright money and the hours left him time to look for Samantha, but sitting with no breaks really sucked ass.

Munching the last of his snack, he tried to decide if he was going to go out tonight or if he should let Saver try, but his phone rang and when he answered it, he was surprised.

"You are a hard man to track down Nick."

"Saver?"

"Yeah, you know it works better if the client leaves contact information before they leave."

"Oh shit," Nick realized the sketch had gotten to him and he had left without leaving his number.

"Yep, but Sam got your sister's file and it was in there. Too bad you don't answer."

"Uh, sorry, just finished my shift with the…"

"Oh yeah, the help desk thing."

"Yeah," Nick dropped onto the couch but he gave it up as a bad idea when his back protested and slid down onto the floor.

"You okay?" asked Xavier in a concerned voice.

"Huh?" Nick said absently as he stretched.

"Are you hurt?" Xavier emphasized each word.

"No, I'm fine," he said confused.

"You groaned like you were hurt, just checking."

"Oh, sorry man, my back is killing me. Just lying on the floor, letting things settle to where they are supposed to be."

"Ah, okay."

"So do you have anything - any news or whatever?"

"I have some news, we found out who took over Leister's turf and I know where to find them, it's a pair of brothers from what I'm told."

"Great," Nick said trying to decide if two were better than one.

"Yeah, they work out of this strip club on Perry."

"Okay," randomly running through clubs that he could think of.

"The Pyramid Club, hear of it?"

"Yeah, in passing, that's all."

" 'K, well not a good place to go."

"All right." Nick said his heart sinking, he was never going to find his sister.

"I'm going to head over tonight and take a swing at Ford."

"You can't find my sister if you're in jail for assaulting a cop."

"I'm not going to hit him, just intimidate the hell out of him."

"Hm."

"Anyway, I'm going to take Melissa out tomorrow and try a few of the clubs."

"Honestly, I'm afraid it's too late, I'm afraid she's gone."

"If she is, we will find her and bring her to your parents," Saver said softly.

"Thank you, Xavier, thank you." Nick hung up quickly trying again not to cry. "Damn it, what is with these people? All I want to do is ball like a bad chick movie?" Deciding he wanted something more than an apple, Nick put on his shoes and grabbed his keys.

CHAPTER EIGHT

Walking into the diner, Melissa waited to be seated and then waited for her waiter to show up to take her order. Looking out the window, she saw Nickolas walk past, as her waiter showed up finally.

"Hey, that guy that just came in, will you show him to this table?" The waiter walked away mumbling about how it wasn't his job and blue haired freaks.

Nick followed the waiter to the table and stopped when he showed him to a table with a blue haired girl sitting at it.

"Uh, wait, blue. What..what happened to the green?"

"Got bored."

"Oh." Nick said sitting at the table. The waiter dropped another menu between them and shook his head as the water stalked off. He picked it up and tried to decide what he wanted to eat.

He found the blue color too distracting. It had made Melissa's eyes stand out even more. The blue should have over-powered the pale powder blue of her eyes but it didn't. Over the top of the laminated menu, Nick watched Melissa. Her eyes darted up and down the plastic, lingered and darted again. She had it tipped back enough that and he could see her lips. Every time her eyes lingered, her tongue would snake out and lick her lips, the pink was a good contrast against the maroon lipstick she wore.

"Have my face memorized yet?"

Nick blinked and cleared his throat "No, but I do like what I see." he said as a peace offering.

"Good, I do too."

Nick squirmed on the vinyl seat, "Uh, good." He had been watching her and hadn't noticed she had been watching him back.

"I learned a long time ago to look without looking, Nick. It was a survival tactic."

"Oh, uh, ah, why did you have it?"

Stopping the conversation before it could start, Melissa said, "Don't ask."

"All right."

Melissa didn't want to lie to Nick, just like she didn't want to lie to Christophe, but neither needed to know about her past.

The waiter came over and took their order for nachos and a ham and cheese omelet.

Trying to make conversation, Nick asked, "So what did you do with your impromptu day off?"

Melissa managed not to choke on her water, but just barely. "Not much," she said nonchalantly. "A little of this, a little of that, got my hair done, saw an old friend."

Raising an eyebrow, Nick said, "Sounds fun and vague at the same time."

"Yeah well, son of a bitch, leave me alone, Aniello," hitting ignore again.

"He's persistent, should I worry about being seen with you?"

Melissa couldn't stop her reaction fast enough. Her head jerked up and she said "No," a lot more harshly than she had meant to. "I'm tired of hiding from him."

Nick sat as far back in his booth as he could.

Melissa dropped her head and sighed, "I'm sorry Nick, I hid from him half my life and I won't do it again, this is my life, not his."

"Ok, all right. So do you know why he keeps calling?"

"No."

"Doesn't he leave a message or anything?"

"Delete them before they play."

"Ah, can't you block his number?"

"He just finds a way to get it unblocked." Melissa said matter-of-factly, as if this was something everyone did.

"Why don't you want to talk to him?"

"Because he's not part of my life and I don't want him to be. Look, can we not talk about Aniello any more please?"

"Sure."

"What did you do today?" Melissa asked attempting to get the conversation away from her, hoping Nick would forget that she hadn't really answered him.

Truthfully, how could she tell him she took a bath fantasizing about him, then got her hair colored while wearing nothing under her skirt, and then went to a bondage club and let herself be dominated by a fuck buddy.

Though it honestly shouldn't matter, they weren't dating or anything. Sure, she found him attractive but she was sure that he wasn't going to be starting a relationship while his sister was missing.

"Worked, nothing fun, your day had to be much more interesting."

This time she did choke.

"Oh god, are you ok? Shit, here, here." Nick grabbed all the napkins he could find to soak up the water Melissa spilled when she coughed up the water she had tried to drink. Then another patron showed up with a large stack of napkins and a soft smile. "Hope your girlfriend's ok."

"Uh yeah, thanks, she'll be fine, just forgot how to drink for a second."

Walking away the lady said, "Shouldn't ask a woman a question while she's drinking."

"Ha! Yeah, I guess," turning back to Melissa, nick said, "Sorry, are you all right?"

"Yeah, yeah." Melissa said, coughing a few more times and taking a small drink of Nick's water.

"I didn't mean to make you choke."

"It's all right, Nickolas, its fine."

"You don't have to tell me about your day, I just figured you really didn't want to hear about mine."

"Your day is fine, Nick. I just don't want to talk about mine."

"There are a lot of things you don't want to talk about."

"Yeah, there are. Look, it's getting late and I want to go home and change before trying a couple clubs."

"I thought Saver wasn't going tonight?"

"He's not, but I can start asking around."

"Is it safe?" Nick asked suddenly concerned.

"Nick, it's safer for me to ask than you."

"But I'm a guy."

"Nick, I have three black belts and have been trained in self-defense since I was old enough to hurt someone. I can handle myself."

"Still, maybe I should go with you."

"You've been there so many times and found nothing. Take a night off, rest, let someone help you."

Nick sat and thought for a moment. "Yeah, I suppose I could use a full night of sleep."

"See, there you go."

"But you could too," Nick countered.

"I slept before I got my hair done and I really only need a few hours."

"Are you sure?" he said, feeling guilty about sleeping while someone else was looking for his sister.

"Yes, Nickolas, go home and sleep."

"If you're positive?"

"Yes."

CHAPTER NINE

Hours later found Nick on his bed trying to sleep. Except every time he closed his eyes he saw midnight blue hair with pale blue eyes and smelled black cherry lip-gloss. When they had left the restaurant, Melissa had hugged him and rushed off. He had watched her, baffled at how she could run in those huge boots, but his attention was yanked away from her feet, by the glint of gold flashing from under her skirt. Nick had blinked and shook his head and looked again but still saw it.

Shaking his head again, he had turned toward his car and caught the scent of her lip-gloss on the shoulder of his jacket. For some reason it had made him hard as hell. Now at home in bed, he couldn't sleep, the scent kept coming back to him. He finally gave up the pretense of trying to sleep, he grabbed his coat, and laid it on the pillow next to him.

Closing his eyes again, he rubbed himself through his shorts and moaned.

"God damn it, this is crazy," he shoved the fabric down and off and pulled on his hardening dick. Nick wondered if Melissa was pale head to toe and that brought him to the thought of what color her pussy might be.

Hissing at the sudden surge of blood to his cock, Nick wondered if the flash of gold he had seen was jewelry and if she had been sitting across from him commando. "Do they call it commando for girls?" He said a loud.

"Oh fuck," he breathed deeply and picked up the pace but stopped and rolled over. He reached for the bottle in the nightstand on the other side of the bed. Rolling back, he popped the bottle open and poured a generous amount onto his cock, hissed again and bucked. "Fuck, fuck, fuck," jacking himself, he let his mind wander, seeing Melissa there with him, kneeling over his cock, leaning farther down until she took him in her mouth and swallowed him all the way to the root.

His eyes flew open at his fantasy, "Oh hell, what am I doing?" he gritted out but didn't make himself stop. Closing his eyes again, she was naked now, her nipples pierced and connected with a chain to a belly piercing. She turned around, looked at him over her shoulder, and winked. Looking her over, he saw a flash of gold again but couldn't tell what it was. His fantasy had provided enough stimulation though, and when she turned back around, he came. "Melissa, oh god, Melissa."

A few minutes later, Nick turned his head away from his jacket and tried to build the energy to get up and clean himself off.

Finally, he managed and stumbled into the bathroom, deciding it would be easier just to take a shower; he turned the water on and stepped in. Leaning against the wall for support, Nick let the water wash over him and shivered. "Damn it, I don't want to." But it had been so long since his body had had any relief; he was still hard and throbbing.

"Damn it." Knowing he would never get to sleep, he braced against the side of the tub and the back wall. Taking his still hard cock in his hand, he was glad he was still slippery with lube, and he began jacking off again. Once more closing his eyes, Melissa was there. This time her hair was green and she was on his bed, legs spread before him. One hand was rubbing her delicate folds while she writhed slowly. Gasping he stepped up the tempo and almost slipped, giving up the idea of standing, he slid down the wall, the water hitting him in the chest, stinging. Adding the pain from the cooling slices, Nick jerked faster and felt a hand glide up his leg to cover his hand. The ghost touch startled him, but he didn't stop, there was a quick twist of his nipple and he came again seeing black for a moment.

Breathing heavily, he grabbed the edge of the tub and the washcloth rack and pulled himself up. Then he waited for the blood to stop rushing all over the place in his body. When the world stopped being grey, he shook his head waited for the world to un-grey a third time. Finally able to stand without holding onto something, he washed off.

After he got and was drying off, Nickolas saw something that wasn't there before, a nail scrape mark on the inside of his thigh where the ghost touch had been.

***

Giving up for the night, Melissa went home. She had tried Sundry and one of the other Goth clubs. She figured she wouldn't get anything but at least she tried, and she had stayed away from Nick for the night, the bigger challenge. Collapsing into her bed, she sighed heavily. It had been hard not to ask him to come to her place, something she had never done before.

No one ever came here, she would go to their place, or they would end up at MINE! using one of the rooms. Some days she felt like a hooker, as she imagined Samantha felt. Of course, she never took money from the people she let fuck her, but more often than not she felt empty and more alone lying next to them than if she hadn't gone out at all.

Undoing the buckles of her skirt, she flung it across the room. Her shirt quickly followed, some asshole had spilled his drink on her.

Getting up, she turned on the water to the shower and stepped in leaning against the wall. She closed her eyes and Nick flashed in front of her. He was strong and vulnerable at the same time. Nickolas was a lost soul and her soul cried out to him. A laugh bubbled up when she thought how corny that sounded, she didn't know him, but damn it, she wanted to.

"Why am I horny again? Fuck. Where's Christophe when I want him? Shit, I don't want Christophe, I want Nick," scraping her nails up her inner thigh and pushing her finger between her lips. She put one leg up on the edge of the bathtub and rubbed her clit, over and over, she pulled at the clip attached to her clit but not hard enough to pull it off. The tension built in her belly and at the last moment, she pulled her nipple ring and came, the world graying out. When the world came back, she washed off and got out.

Drying off, she looked to see how badly she had scratched herself and found only a faint red line. Shrugging, she climbed into bed, and shivered as a final wave of aftermath rolled over her. She closed her eyes and was asleep before she took her next breath.

CHAPTER TEN

Saver stood outside of a club waiting for Melissa to show up, they had agreed on 10:30. It was 10:50, a tap on his shoulder had him turning and grabbing the hand.

"Saver, hey, hey, sorry, forgot."

"Shit, Mel."Xavier growled releasing her arm.

Melissa didn't complain about the name as she shook blood back into her arm.

"I'm sorry sweetie, I shouldn't have a…" Saver started to apologize.

"No, I know better than to come up behind you."

"I can't overreact like that though."

"Saver," Melissa said pulling the big Marine into a hug, "it's okay. I understand." Xavier had been a POW and tortured. He was much better about being around people since meeting Emiko, one of the sisters she never had, but he still had flashbacks and panic attacks.

"Maybe this isn't a good idea for you. Maybe we should call Sam."

Shaking his head, "No, I need to do this."

"Honey, this doesn't have to be emersion therapy. You don't have to jump into the deep end of the pool when you've just taken off the floaties."

"Oh god, Melissa." he said hugging her back. "No, I can do this, I will do this, and it can't be that bad."

"Oh babe, you don't know what you're getting yourself into." Standing up as straight as she could, Melissa took a deep breath and did her best attempt to sound like a drill sergant. "Marine, put your hands in your pocket and don't take them out unless I say otherwise. Do you understand?"

Raising an eyebrow, Saver did what she asked and nodded. "Good, now your mission tonight is to infiltrate this club and get intel on one Samantha Todd aka Janie. Do you accept?"

"Was never an option, Mel." Saver said deadpan.

"Whatever, spoil all my fun." Melissa said using her own voice and sounding slightly hurt.

"I know what you're doing sweetie, and thank you." Xavier said placing a kiss on her forehead. "Come on, let's head out LT."

"LT?"

"Lieutenant."

"Oooouuuh a promotion."

Shaking his head, Xavier held back asking; he wasn't sure he wanted to know what that meant.

***

Walking into the club, Melissa saw a few faces she knew but not well enough to approach. Wandering toward the bar, she felt Xavier jump and decided that maybe he should take point. She was trying to get into the whole military special ops mindset. She stopped, turned, and found Saver's face dark and tormented. "Saver, hey, Saver you're here, not back there. You're here with me remember?"

"I know, I'm okay, I'm fine."

"How about you go first and, and, I'll watch your six. That's the right term, right? I'll watch your back."

"Yeah, six is right."

"Okay, you take point and I've got your six." She said touching his arm, hoping to remind him he was safe. She hadn't seen him have a flashback but she heard about them from Emiko and Cassandra. It wasn't something she wanted to see. So walking as close as she could to him without stepping on his heels, they made their way to the bar. She swatted at a few hands that had tried to grope his ass but most made their way to her ass.

"What do you want?" Xavier asked over his shoulder.

"Tell her a 'Melissa'." She received another eyebrow raise and a headshake but he passed on the information with his order for water.

"I should tell you that the water here is worse than death." Melissa warned him.

"Great."

"Bring one of your handy little deacon packs, solider boy?" Melissa asked. She knew she was baiting the tiger but hey, better to live dangerously than not to live at all. Instead of Saver snapping her head off, he choked on his water and laughed.

"Solider boy. Do I look like a boy to you?"

"No, but hey if the shoe fits."

"Well it doesn't. Not a soldier and not a boy." The look on Savers face made her heart hurt. He had lost his friends, when they really were no more than boys, he still wasn't over it but he was getting better.

"I'm sorry Saver, I was just teasing."

"It's fine, Mel, I'm fine."

"Should we do this so we can get you out of here?"

"I'm not broken, I'm just..."

"Just hate places with more than a few people in it." Melissa finished for him.

"Have to learn to deal if I'm going to do this kind of thing."

"I know, I know, I feel rotten for getting you into this when you aren't quite ready though," Melissa said, her face almost as sad as Xavier's.

"I'm good to go, who should we bug first?"

"Jasper."

"Okay, lead on McDuff."

"No, you head toward the white door and I'll follow behind," still trying to keep Saver safe.

He chuckled but did as she said. Once at the door Melissa glared daggers at everyone near the door until they backed off a few steps and then she knocked. They only had to wait a few seconds before it opened and a large black man blocked the doorway, "What you want little girl?"

"Tiny, you got to let me talk to Jasper. I need to know if he knows about a missing girl."

"Girly, I don't got to nothen."

"Man, Tiny, get laid would ya? I need in." Melissa said, shoving the behemoth man out of her way.

"Littlen, I'm gonna knock you out."

"I wouldn't try it if I were you, Tiny." Saver said in full protector mode. The way he said 'Tiny' made it sound like the man was 4 foot nothing instead of 6'11 and 350 pounds.

Melissa and Tiny both laughed. "Sorry, Saver. Tiny and I go way back. He's just messing with me. If he didn't want to move when I pushed him, he wouldn't have moved. I'm good but not that good."

"Melissa, if you're going to go with me to these clubs, can I have that kind of intel beforehand? Before I hurt someone I don't need to. It's hell for Sam to fill out the paper work." Xavier said with a heavy sigh.

"Sorry sweetie, I'll try to say something, but I thought this big lug was on VACATION WITH HIS HONEY!" Melissa yelled.

Tiny ducked his head and shuffled his feet, "Little man left me."

"WHAT?" Melissa almost screeched, "Is he stupid, you're the best person in the world for him. Damn it, what happened?"

"Later littlen, later. I think your man's not interested," Tiny said tipping his head toward the doorway.

"Well shit, Saver," Melissa said walking over to the slightly zoned marine. "Hey big guy, you good? You ok?" Knowing better then to touch him, she just talked. "Hey Xavier."

Thinking to herself Melissa asked, *'Damn it, what set this off man?'*

"I need you here, remember?"

And as suddenly as Saver's fugue started, it ended. "Sorry, damn it, shit, fuck, damn."

"It's okay man, here," Tiny said to the man, handing him a bottle of water and clasping a large hand on his shoulder guiding him to a couch after he kicked the door closed with his massive shoe.

"Fuck. Fuck." Taking a deep breath and a deep drink of water, "I'm good, I'm fine."

"Are you sure? You're still pale, Saver," Melissa asked, as shaken as her friend.

"Yeah, Melissa, I'm fine, just need a second."

"Gulf?" Tiny asked.

Saver shook his head and looked up at the big man; seeing a Ranger tattoo showing from under the sleeve of his shirt, Xavier said "Afghanistan."

"Just as bad."

"Pretty much."

After a few minutes, Saver stood and downed the rest of the water, "Let's talk to this Jasper."

"About what?" asked a small man, leaning against the doorframe.

Melissa turned and said, "Jasper, you are worse than the vamp wannabe's around here."

"No, I'm better."

Melissa laughed and said, "Yep, Saver needs to ask you something."

Saver took the sketch from his pocket and handed it to the pale little man with white hair.

"We are looking for this woman. She's in her thirties, she is...has...well.."

"Janie," Jasper said. "It's Janie."

"Yeah, that's her name, her um, other name." Melissa stuttered.

"She's a call girl I know. Who's looking for her?"

"Her brother. He hasn't seen her in over a month and he's really worried."

Jasper sat down and looked at the drawing, "I haven't seen her in about.." pausing to think, "Tiny, when did the line break for the soda?"

"Was three weeks and, um, four days." He said after a minute.

"It was three weeks and three days ago."

"How can you be so sure?" Saver asked.

"Janie was here the night it broke and then the next night as well. She usually doesn't come two nights in a row. That's how I can know for sure."

"But you're sure she hasn't been back since?" Xavier pushed.

"Yes, I'm sure, she always stops and gets a sucker from me."

"Wait, a sucker?"

Melissa put her hand on Savers arm. "Jasper is a daddy to a lot of people here. A dad, not some sicko, he listens to us and we, well, most of us are a sort of family."

"I know about Janie's line of work and I know about her addiction to more than my watermelon Tootsie pops. I have tried to talk her into getting help. I've given her numbers of every group I can think of, every center, hospice, rehab, everything. I have missed seeing her because at least I knew she was ok, but she's gone weeks without stopping by before. I was beginning to worry but I hoped she would come in this week."

"Okay, so," Xavier started to pace the room. "Nick saw her six weeks, four days ago and you saw her three weeks ago. She was out but she didn't stop at her brother's and she didn't call, why?"

"She was here both nights and she stopped by but she didn't stay and talk with me. She was very jumpy, like she kept waiting for someone to bust in. And she had the scar on her chin." He said, tapping the sketch.

Xavier shivered, "Damn, she was right." He mumbled.

"Usually is." Melissa said, "So she was here and doing her routine but wasn't herself."

"Yes." Jasper said nodding "She knew I would know she was here and come to her if she didn't stop by, so she came here to avoid me."

"How would you know she was here?"

"Camera on the entrance." Tiny said, "He sees everyone."

"Well, wouldn't you have seen who she came in with then?"

"Yes and no. I see everyone who comes in, but if they came in separately, I wouldn't know if they got together once they were in the club. I don't have cameras on the floor. My children," everyone but Saver laughed, "are not always the most well behaved individuals. So if I don't tape it, I can't be made to tell on them and they keep coming and talking to me and I am able to help them more."

"What about crime, robberies and..."

"They don't happen at Sundry, Saver, cameras or not, they don't happen. Everyone who would come here knows Jasper, and the ones who would do that kind of thing stay away, because they know about the security staff too," Melissa explained.

"So you do have security?"

"Of course, I love my children; I do not want them hurt. The ones who come here know who in the crowd is there to help, and the ones that don't, would never look, so they don't know they are watched until the pavement is under their asses. In ten years, Sundry has had only one violent crime, in the men's room and there was no way any of our staff could have gotten there in time. It was a fight over a dropped lighter of all things."

"Okay, so Sundry is safe. Do you keep tapes of the entrance?"

"Yes, but only for two weeks."

"Well shit," Saver cursed.

"I'm sorry. I will make a few calls and see if anyone has seen or heard about Janie."

"Thank you, Jasper," Melissa said, hugging the little man and then pulling the head off of a dragon cookie jar on the corner of the desk. Looking in and smiling she pulled a chocolate tootsie pop and un-wrapped it. "See you."

"I'll see you first."

"As always," she sang back as she and Saver left the office. Tiny followed out and opened the door to the club floor.

"You will call me when you get up and you will tell me what has gotten into Rock."

"Yes ma'am."

Reaching up as high as she could Melissa hugged the giant black bear and kissed him on the cheek when he bent down to her level.

CHAPTER ELEVEN

Hours later found Xavier and Melissa at the coffee shop she had taken Nick to. "Oh my god, this is so frustrating. I wish I had talked to Nick the first night he talked to me."

"When was that?" Xavier wondered out loud.

"Three days after the last person saw Samantha. Damn it, if I had called you that night instead of two nights ago you would have, uh.." pausing for a second "fresh leads."

"Melissa, we will find her."

"I know, but still it's so frustrating. Nick said she would never go back to a pimp, but I would guess from the way people are talking about her that she has someone pulling her strings."

Xavier sat for a little while drinking his coffee "I think you're right, I think someone has her under their control but I don't think it's a pimp. I think it's going to be her drug dealer. This Lasiter guy sounds like, oh man, this is going to sound nuts, but a decent dealer."

"Yeah, that's strange."

"He didn't cut his stuff with things that would kill his clients. He, man, he took care of them because in the end they took care of him. One guy we talked to yesterday said Lasiter got him a job, he kept buying from him but it was 'cause he had the job. He bought less because he liked his job and wanted to keep it but he still got high so Lasiter kept him as a client."

"Man, this is a screwed up world."

"Yeah, I know this guy also said he got clean when Lasiter went up because the two that took over don't give a shit, and he heard they were cutting their heroin with junk, and that it wasn't good quality stuff to begin with. He said that honestly, if Lasiter got out tomorrow and was selling, he would get high again but as long as Lasiter was up he was clean."

Melissa shook her head and drank her mocha. "So the newbies are dirty sleaze and the oldie was clean sleaze."

"Yep, ok, so let's think, where haven't we hit that she might be?" Xavier questioned.

Melissa thought for a while. She knew one place but she didn't want to go there with anyone. There was no way she could hide that she had been there before and no way for her not to stand out, it was what she did for Christ sake.

"Melissa?" Xavier said her name trying to get her attention. he did not like the look on her face, he seen it a time or two in the mirror.

'How can I take Xavier to MINE! It would never work.' Lost in her own thoughts she didn't hear the marine calling her name.

"Melissa, did you hear me?"

'If I went to blond, maybe, no no, not doing that'…still lost in her own inner turmoil.

"Melissa." Xavier reached out and poked her in the arm. "Hey, earth to Melissa, you in there? Thought I was the only one that got to get spacey."

"No, I'm here, sorry, I was just thinking."

"What about, Pluto?"

"No MINE!"

"Mine, what, you have your coffee, I didn't touch it," Xavier said seriously confused.

"No, not mine," she sighed "MINE! It's a club."

"Okay let's go."

"I can't go with you, Xavier."

"What do you mean?" his confusion only getting worse.

"Let me see if Nick can go with me," she said quickly.

"Melissa, what is MINE!?"

"It's a club, but not one I can or will take you into."

"Melissa, I know you can handle your..."

"It's not that, Saver, it's just, it's my place to go when I need..." trailing off unable to tell him.

"Need what?" Xavier asked warily.

'To get my brains fucked out or to fuck someone's brains out, where I go to

get tied up and paddled,' she thought to herself.

"Melissa, you're zoning again."

"No I'm not. I don't want to, oh for fucking Christ sake." Pulling her phone from her pocket, she opened it and yelled into it, "No, hell no, no, no, no, leave me alone," and hung up.

"Melissa, what is going on?" Saver demanded.

"Nothing. Look, it's been a long night, I'm going home. I'll check MINE! tomorrow with Nick. You and Sam can do the other cop-ie things and I'll call you when I get done."

"Melissa, who was on the phone?"

"She said it was her godfather." Nick said from behind her. Her midnight hair flung around as she whirled to look at him.

"Shouldn't sneak up on people," she accused.

"Didn't sneak, Saver saw me."

"I'm sure he did." Melissa grumbled getting up, "I'm going home."

"I'll walk you." Nick and Saver said at the same time.

"No, I'll walk myself."

"No you won't missy." Xavier said gruffly.

"Damn it, Saver you have no idea what I can handle, so back the hell off." Melissa snapped and shoved Xavier back down into his chair before storming out the door.

Nick said, "I'll call you when I know she's home," and ran out after her.

"Melissa, are you okay?" He said calling ahead to her.

"No, I'm not."

"Did I say something?" Nick asked.

"No," Melissa stopped, "it's not you, well sort of, not really, oh fuck," she kicked a can on the sidewalk and watched it skitter into an alley.

"Two points."

"Thanks."

"So what is MINE! and why am I going instead of your brother?"

"MINE! is a bondage club and you're going because he is my brother."

"Ah, okay, and I'm going to guess that none of your family knows about that side of you?"

"Knows, no, suspects, maybe, and I would like to leave it like that. Can you handle it if we go and your sister is there?"

"Yes." Nickolas said with complete confidence.

"Look, shit, maybe I'll, no, yeah, no, you should go. I'll call Christophe - what I am saying? I don't need anyone, I'll just go."

"No, look, Xavier told me about the two that have taken over for Samantha's dealer. They are not nice, so if they have her they are not going to let her go just because you say so."

"And like they're going to because you did?" Melissa shouted.

"Look, you're a woman, they obviously don't respect women." He yelled back.

"Yeah, I get that."

"No one wants you to get hurt."

"I can take care of myself. GOD DAMN IT! ANIELLO STOP CALLING ME," she yelled into the phone before slapping it closed yet again.

While arguing, the pair had walked most of the way to Melissa's house. Now she stopped and took several deep breaths, "Nick, I grew up in a very harsh environment, my father was killed because of it. I have known how to take care of myself since I was eight. I don't need anyone to take care of me," pushing the key into her lock.

Nick grabbed her arm and spun her around, "No, you don't need anyone to do anything for you. I can see that, but sometimes it's nice if someone else does something for you anyway." He leaned in, pinning her to her own front door. "Your scent has driven me crazy for weeks."

And then he kissed her.

CHAPTER TWELVE

And she kissed him back.

Somehow, the pair made it inside. Nick's hand was fisted into Melissa's hair, he pulled her head back and kissed her deeper. Melissa moaned and shivered. A moment later, she felt herself being picked up and pinned to the inside of her front door. Nick let go of her hair and then both hands were on her ass caressing and kneading. His hand slid up her leg to her stockings, he found the hook to her garter and unhooked it. Shifting her weight so he had one hand free he untied her boot but when he tried to take it off, he found that he couldn't.

"It's a two hand operation," she said breaking the kiss and leaning her head back against the door.

"I see that, I'm afraid to put you down though."

"Why?" Melissa said breathlessly.

"I'm afraid you'll come to your senses and kick me out the door."

"Oh no buddy, you pushed the button and now you've got to pay the toll."

Kissing her, he set her on her feet, Nick let go and knelt to the floor.

"Now there's a good place for you," she said huskily looking down at him.

"Not too bad if I do say so myself," Nick replied looking up, as close as he was he could clearly see Melissa's panties matched her hair, what little fabric there was. Kissing the inside of her thigh he finished untying the other boot and Melissa steadied herself using his shoulder as she stepped out of her boots one at a time. Once they were off, Nick reached up, unhooked the second stocking, and rolled it down her leg scraping his nails on her leg as he went. Melissa hissed and arched her back in response. "Mmm, just like a cat."

"Sometimes," Melissa moaned.

While still kneeling, Nick rose up, he was only a few inches shorter than Melissa was now that the boots were gone. She tipped her head and he kissed her again. Gliding his hands up and over her ass, he brought the back of her skirt with him.

Walking her back a few steps, he pinned her to the wall. "So if I wanted to get rid of this scrap of fabric, how would I do it?" he whispered into her neck.

"Buckles on the side," she answered arching her back again.

"Hmm, maybe I'll leave it, maybe I won't, I'll decide later," Nick said as he kissed his way from the waistband of her skirt up, taking her shirt up as he went. Pulling it over her head he dropped it to the ground behind him, then leaned back taking in the debauched beauty in front of him. "You look like one of those hentai girls, all sexy and blue."

Melissa laughed, "And only my demi bra and skirt on."

"Oh wait, they never have these on," he said, pulling her panties down and off, "course there's so little to them."

"Hardly worth the bother," Melissa whispered huskily.

Adding them to the pile behind him, he nodded "Hardly," sliding his hand back up her leg and under the skirt. "What is this?" he said when he felt something brush across the top of his knuckles.

"Oh, uh, that, those are..."

"You have your clit pierced?" Nick gasped.

"No, no, it's not pierced."

"Really? Your nipples are, I can see those," reaching up and sliding the left cup down and under her breast. Pulling lightly on the slender ring, he heard Melissa moan again then purred. "So much like a kitty."

Sliding his thumb over her clit, he heard her hiss and felt the jewelry sway. "Oh god," Unbuckling the first buckle, he reached for the second when her phone rang. "What is that?" he asked.

"That would be Xavier calling, it's the Marine's hymn."

"That is the weirdest version I've ever heard." Nick commented dropping his head on to the wall behind her.

"That's 'cause it's an electric guitar version." Pulling her phone from a pocket in her skirt she said, "Yes dad, I'm home, Nick walked me *all the way* to my door.

No, I'm fine. No, I will not discuss it right now, I'm busy. No, I won't tell you what I'm doing. No, Saver, I'm fine, more than fine. In a little while if you are a good friend and hang up right now. Good bye."

"Halls of Montezuma on an electric guitar, hmm, that works."

"No symphony for Saver, not his style."

"Nope, it's not," Nick smiled up at Melissa, "now where was I?"

"You had your thumb on my clit, is where you were..." but was interrupted when he returned his hand to where it was before the call.

"Oh that's right, like this?" he asked teasingly when instead of on her clit he pushed two fingers into her pussy.

"Oh, not quite, but it will do quite nicely instead."

"Thought so."

"Bloody hell," Melissa whimpered when her phone rang again, still in her hand. She flipped it over, popped the back off and flicked the battery out and across the room, throwing the phone onto her stool she pulled away from Nick. "Let's take this to the bedroom."

"Hmm sounds good." Reaching over and knocking her legs out from under her, Nick caught Melissa and said, "Which way, my lady?"

Melissa laughed and told him "Down the hall, only door on the left."

Walking into the room, Melissa put her hand on the doorjamb making Nick stop. She felt on the wall for the light switch and then the room was bathed in a warm glow of blue light.

"So you always match?" Nick asked when he looked around. Her curtains were blue as were the sheets and the robe that hung off one of the four bedposts.

"Hmm, most of the time."

"And blue panties too."

"Well yeah, those always match."

Setting her on the bed, Nick finished with her buckles and pulled the skirt off of her, "Hmm, I see you have bare floors," commenting on her shaved pussy.

"Never have to worry about the carpet not matching the curtains that way," Melissa countered.

Looking Melissa over, Nick took in a sharp breath. Her hair fanned out above her was a stark contrast to the pale blue comforter she lay on. The light cast a blue hue across her that made her skin almost match her pillows. Her nipples were pierced and a dainty chain hung between them he hadn't noticed it before.

"Take your bra off," he ordered. Leaning up, Melissa did as he asked. "Lay back," again she did as he said. The chain was free of her bra and glittered in the light, both nipples were hard and pointed and with every breath she took the stones in the rings shimmered.

Now that the skirt was gone, he saw that she had a belly chain on also; it was of the same style as the chain at her breasts.

"Open your legs," He said hoarsely.

Doing one better, Melissa raised her knees up 'till her feet were flat on the bed and let her legs fall open.

Nick couldn't breathe.

Before him, he could see what had brushed against his hand earlier, and something that had been teasing his memory for days. Un-buttoning his shirt he spoke softly, "So when you left the diner the other day you weren't wearing any panties? You know how I know this?" Not waiting for her to answer, Nick continued as he dropped his shirt to the floor. "I know this because I saw your lovely little ass jewelry. See, I thought I was seeing things, but if your panties always match your hair then I should have seen blue. But I didn't, I saw gold. Now the clip on your clit is silver with blue stones and I'm betting if I had seen you naked last week it would have been silver with green stones."

"Yes," Melissa whispered.

"You go out in public often without panties?"

"No, not often," She squirmed under the attention and the question, remembering what had happened that day.

"Just when you get your hair done?"

"Hmmm, only when I don't know what color I'm getting it done."

Nick crawled up the bed and kissed Melissa silent. "Does that little clip help you come or keep you from coming?" Nick whispered into the kiss.

"Hmm, makes it last longer."

"Really, what about the little gold one, what does it do?"

"Makes me feel wicked and naughty all day."

"Well, well, do you like feeling wicked?"

"God yes," Melissa said as she bolted up from the bed pushing Nick down.

"Ah," Before Nick could react; Melissa was sucking his cock into her mouth.

"Oh god," Nick let the feeling of her tongue on his cock wash over him for a few minutes but the need to hear her purr again grew, "No, stop, oh god, did I just say that?"

"Yes, you did," pulling away far enough to speak.

"Okay stop, but only because I want to be in you."

"Oh, that can be arranged," Melissa said, taking his cock in her in one fluid motion.

"Yes," they said simultaneously.

When their skin touched, they both sighed. "Oh hell, you feel so damn good; oh man, I shouldn't tell you this but it's been a while."

"Why you're a handsome guy, you could have taken home any girl or guy from any of the clubs."

"I couldn't, I was too worried about Samantha."

"We'll find her."

"I know," pulling her down to him, Nick kissed Melissa, and thrust into her and was rewarded with a purr.

"Hmm, little pussy purrs just like a little kitty."

"Only if you pet her right, otherwise she turns into a big tiger that can tear you to pieces."

"I bet," thrusting again pulling her hair into his hand, Melissa gasped and then cried in surprise as Nick rolled them over putting him on top. "I'm going to make you purr nemnogo kotenok."

"Hmm, don't know what you just said but it sounds pretty."

"I'll tell you later," kissing her silent Nickolas thrust again, setting a pace that didn't allow for any more talking.

A few minutes later Nick felt his orgasm building; he growled to himself, he didn't want to stop. Melissa felt so good but just as he was about to change positions to prolong their sex, he felt Melissa quiver and it pulled him impossibly close. He heard his little kitten purr again and then he heard her cry out. This time when her pussy quivered, it pushed him over the edge and he was crying out as well.

"Mmmmm, now what was it you said before?" Melissa asked sometime later.

"Huh?" Nick tried to lift his head off Melissa's chest but couldn't. "What, man I've melted, I can't move."

"Yeah, you melted alright," she said wagging an eyebrow.

"Oh hey, that's hitting below the belt."

"I know."

"Alright, what did you ask?" Nick said sliding off Melissa and onto the bed and his back.

"I asked what you said before."

"Um, uh, ah, oh, I called you my little kitten, you know keeping up the whole purring theme."

"Ah, I do purr a lot don't I?" She said stretching.

"Yeah and you seem to stretch like one to."

"Thank you."

"Ne za chto."

"What language is that?"

"Russkij jazyk"

"Okay buster," Melissa said rolling onto her side and then pouncing on Nick, she started to tickle him and when he curled into the fetal position she knew she had a weapon, "you better cut that out and…"

"Ahhhhh! I give, I give, it's Russian, yah...quit, quit, I give!" Nick cried breathless in between fits of laughter.

"Alright, I'll quit," Melissa said when she noticed he was a little pale and his breathing was as hard as it had been just before he came.

Bouncing off the bed, she walked into her bathroom, grabbed a towel, and threw it at him before shutting the door.

Lying on the bed, Nick cleaned himself off and caught his breath. "When was the last time I felt so rested and so happy? When was the last time I laughed?" He asked himself.

"Talking to yourself?"

"Yeah, sorry."

"It's okay, I do it too."

Surprised he answered, "Really, always drove everyone nuts."

"Yep, know the feeling. So you speak Russian?"

"Yeah, my mother was Russian, she spoke it at home. I've forgotten a lot though."

"Hm mio padre era italiano dunque abbiamo parlato l'italiano."

"Ahhh, one of the romance languages, obviously Italian."

"Yes. So anyway, sex makes me hungry, I'm going to raid the kitchen. You want anything?"

"Hmm, something to drink, don't care what."

Bouncing off the bed again, Melissa strolled down her hall to the kitchen; she hummed as she searched for something to eat. Pulling ice cream from the freezer and two bottles of water, Melissa stopped in the living room long enough to scoop up her battery and cell. Returning to the bedroom, she found Nickolas in the bathroom washing up with his jeans on.

"Water," she offered.

"Thanks, ouu, ice cream, does the kotenok share?"

"Is that the word for kitten?"

"Yeah." Nick said shrugging.

"Then yes, the kotenok shares."

"Spasibo."

"Only brought one spoon," Melissa said showing the single piece of silver.

"We can share."

**

After about half the carton was gone Nick asked, "So, this club?"

"MINE!"

"Yeah, you really don't want to take Saver there, do you?"

"No, and for more than one reason."

"Care to enlighten me?" Nick asked, feeding her another bite of ice cream.

"For one, he's still battling his PTSD pretty hard. Small things set it off, someone brushing past him, ah, sometimes... oh hey, don't do the Russian thing in front of him either, that does it pretty hard core."

"How would Russian?"

"No, any foreign language."

"What, why?"

"He was on a mission overseas with his two best friends and they spoke like, uh, crap, I don't remember, like twenty languages, but he was never very good at them, so sometimes he hears something and it sends him back to when they were captured, tortured, and they were killed and he survived, barely. Emiko did it once and he had a serious flashback, like fetal position, and took an hour to come out of it."

"Holy shit."

"Yeah, so stick to English around him."

"Ok, obviously you don't speak Italian around him."

"I don't speak Italian around anyone, but back to the reasons not to take him. The flashback thing, first and foremost; second is, it's not a place you take someone with an exaggerated protective streak."

"'K," Nick said in a tone that meant he got it without getting it.

"It's a heavy bondage club, Nickolas, scenes all over the place, not just in the rooms. You can't do humiliation if no one is around to see you being humiliated."

Nick raised his eyebrows, "Okay."

"And then there's the noise, he's not really good with sudden screams. So a combination of one and two there."

"Right, can see that."

"And lastly, I don't want him to find out," getting up off the bed Melissa paced. "I don't want him to find out how well I'm known there, it's also why I can't take Sam. I don't want my family to know that side of me."

"You don't want them to know about this?" he said reaching over wiggling the dangling chains hanging from her ass.

She stilled for a moment shivered and moaned, "Yeah," she finally strangled out, "I don't want them to know about that."

"Or this?" he said moving his hand to the clip that was still on her clit.

"Or that," she moaned, "damn it, stop."

"No, I like the look on your face."

"If you don't, you'll get all dirty again."

"Fine with me, I clean easily and so do you," he said nibbling on her shoulder.

"But I need sleep, I have to get up and go to work tomorrow," pulling away from Nick, and holding onto the bedpost.

"Is this you kicking me out?"

Melissa's head whipped around as she stopped poking through her drawers trying to find a nightgown, "No, it's me saying I need sleep, if you want to stay you can."

"I think I want to stay," Nick whispered into her ear as his arms snaked around her waist, "you know you are really short?"

Melissa laughed turning in his arms and said, "No, you're just tall. So commando, boxers, or I think I have a pair of sweats that might fit you around here."

"I'll go with my boxers."

"'K," she watched as Nick kicked off his jeans, picked them up, and looked around the room.

"Just put those over the foot board or Mambo will lie on them."

"Mambo?"

"My cat, I'm guessing you're not allergic."

"No, I have one of my own Mammajamma."

"What is it's name?"

"His name is Mammajamma."

"Why?"

"Friend of mine has a cat that walks across his keyboard at really bad times, and his online name is Mammajamma. So when I got this cat and he started to walk on mine, I had to name him Mammajamma, Mamma for short."

"Ah, Mambo is just Mambo, but he will lie on any stray clothing."

"Noted." Nick lay down on the bed but rolled to his side when he heard the closet door open. He watched Melissa pull out a black pleated skirt with a petty coat underneath and pull a couple shirts out. She looked at them. "The silver one," he offered.

"Hmm, a man after my own heart, it was the one I was leaning toward."

Hanging the clothes up on a hook on the outside of the closet Melissa crawled into bed and over the top of Nickolas, so that he was between her and the door, "Sorry, don't sleep next to the door."

"No problems, it's your bed."

"Thanks."

**

Nick jerked awake a few hours later when Melissa's phone rang Godsmack's Voodoo Woman. "Do you have just a plain ring tone on that thing?"

"No," she said answering the phone, "Yes, my lady liege?"

"Yeah, sure, that's fine, nope, I'll just go back to sleep, thanks.

That's why everyone has a ring tone; I know who's calling without looking. That was the boss lady. She wanted to know if I would switch with Anne, she's got a doctor's appointment."

"Ahh, so you get to stay right here?"

"Yep, but you?"

"Don't have to work today, no call center for me."

"Nice."

"Yeah, begged Peter to take this week, so that I could spend more time looking for Samantha."

"Ahh, you're a good brother."

"If I was a good brother I would have done this six weeks ago," Nick said sullenly.

"Hey. Hey, you've been looking, but you've been paying the bills too, man."

"I know, I just…"

"No, you're doing what you can and not lose your life too, now about that sleep," Melissa purred in Nick's ear, "Do you really need it?"

"Hmm," kissing her neck, "No, not really."

CHAPTER THIRTEEN

Hours later Melissa found herself in front of MINE! with Nickolas, after having had a huge argument with both Saver and Sam. To make everything even worse, Aniello called three times while Saver and Sam talked about tying her up. She had to point out that they wouldn't be let past the front door without a warrant and they had no cause to get one.

When they asked why, she had to tell them that it was members and guests only. That hadn't gone over well, then the two had demanded to know why she had a membership, and well...

In the end, they had agreed only after she promised to take a wire and a panic button, and after she agreed to let the two knights sit out in the parking lot waiting to rush in and save her.

She shook her head and said, "Come on, lets go," pulling Nick in behind her. She wanted to lose the mic in so many ways. She knew as soon as she went in she would be greeted like she was every time, and with her luck Marishka would be at the front door waiting for some little nibblette to come in, and this is why she didn't want Saver to come in.

Nick could feel Melissa fidgeting; he was sure she was worried about what the mic would pick up. Cupping his hand over it and whispering in her ear, "Just think of the flashbacks you're saving him from and deal with them finding out about what you like later. They are family, they won't care."

She just nodded and pulled the door open and braced herself for the reaction.

Inside she lucked out, Marishka was not at the door. She was, however, at the bar with a man dressed only in leather pants. Christophe was there, but he didn't see her right away. A few others she knew called out to her but fortunately, it was only to say hi. Nick being with her was definitely toning down her reception. Walking to the backup bar, Melissa ordered her usual drink and looked at Nick, "What do you want?"

"A lime giant," he called out looking at the stage with the bed on it, "dare I ask?"

"No, you don't," she replied taking her drink from the bartender.

"Okay," Nick looked around trying to make sense of what he saw. Men and women with collars and leashes, people in varying degrees of undress. Jewelry attached to everything and everywhere. "This is like some weird…"

"Don't finish that sentence please," Melissa said in a tight voice.

"Okay, I won't."

Just then, her phone went off and she dropped her head to her chest. Pulling it from her pocket, "Yes, Xavier I'm fine. Look, please just turn the thing off. I have the stupid panic button, my cell, my brains, and Nick. I can take care of myself. I knocked you on your ass if you remember," she said snapping her phone closed. "This is stupid," she pulled the pretty pin off her shirt and shoved it in Nick's pocket. "I won't throw it away but

I'm not going to edit what I say either to keep them from finding out."

"Finding out what, my lady?" Christophe said from behind Melissa, leaning in kissing her on the cheek.

Nick saw conflicting emotions play across Melissa's face, surprise, frustration, a love of sorts, and fear. The last was when her eyes landed on him.

"Christophe, I, hi."

Christophe was the boyish looking man that Nick had run into at the clubs and at the precinct the last time he had talked to Ford. "You're.. hey.. I, you..."

"Hmmm, is it something in the drinks tonight, neither one of you can talk?"

Melissa sighed, took a deep breath and said, "We are looking for Nick's sister, Christophe; she's been missing for a long time."

"That why you were so upset that day, the police were not helping you?" the man asked.

"Yeah, Ford was being a dick. My sister.." Nick stopped and looked to

Melissa. The girl was still scared and for some reason Nick felt she wasn't really afraid of much. "Melissa, you ok? You're paler than..."

"Usual," Christophe finished, "even for you." He turned to Nick, "how long have you known Melissa?" he asked, walking them to a booth.

"Uh, well, a few days, but I saw her the first time I saw you."

Melissa finally found her voice, "Chris, I.. we are looking for his sister, Janie. Have you heard anyone in the scene with that name?"

Nick watched again and saw confusion flash on Christophe's face; apparently he didn't use Chris much.

"Well Mel, no, I can't say I have. But I could ask around if you want me to, Mel."

Nick watched Melissa flinch each time Christophe called her Mel. What the hell was going on here. "Melissa, what is going on? I hate being left out like this. I just want to know if I'm in the way of something, or if it's going to cause a problem finding my sister..."

"Melissa has secrets she keeps from everyone," Christophe said after a few minutes of a staring match, "she never tells men anything she doesn't have to, she's a very bad little sub, but then she's not really cut out to be a sub either."

"Damn it, Christophe," Melissa said, trying to get out of the booth but he was faster.

"No Melissa, you want to stay right here. Marishka is around and you know she'll hound you, and if you don't want your little friend to find out about you, you had better be with me."

"Stay here Nick, don't go anywhere, don't talk to anyone, and don't even look at anyone," Melissa said pulling Christophe away.

"Christophe, I'm sorry about this. It has nothing to do with; oh man I'm not hiding things from him. Well, not really, he has a mic and on the other end of the mic is my brother and his best friend who also is a cop. I was trying to keep them from finding out about my life."

"Honey, if he's your brother, don't you think he knows?"

"Not that kind of brother. He's Emiko's fiancée, he's my brother because we all choose to make him a brother."

"Okay, I get it, like Cassandra's James."

"Yeah, most of us are orphans, so we are making our own family."

"Sweet Melissa is afraid to lose her family because she isn't vanilla."

"No, not lose it, just mess it up. I know Cassandra and Yvette could handle it but the other girls are a little more straight and not so bent as I am."

Christophe pulled Melissa to his chest, "Little one, you know anyone who meets you can't help but love you, right? You have this way of sneaking in and moving into people's hearts. Blue, green, pink or blonde hair, I'm betting your brothers and sisters couldn't care less if you like to get tied up or if you've taken a strap on and fucked a guy to oblivion."

Nick stood with Xavier and Sam and hoped that Christophe was right because she had just been outed to the very guys she had been trying to keep in the dark.

Xavier tapped Christophe on the shoulder and pulled Melissa from his arms. "We don't care, Melissa. We only wanted you to be safe in here. If you had told us that this was a place you came often we wouldn't have worried, but all the secrets and silence worried us."

"Look kid, I don't care what you do so long as you are safe." Sam put his hand on her shoulders, "you're a niece to me."

"You guys, no one's ever wanted for me what I wanted for me. I've always had to hide what I did and wanted."

"No more secrets, there have been too many. They can mess you up, bad, Melissa," Xavier whispered to her, "Trust a guy who knows."

"Well this is so cute I think I'll just go puke," Marishka said, leaning against a nearby doorjamb. "Melissa, get your ass out of the middle of all those men and come with me now."

Melissa put a calming hand on Xavier's arm as the marine turned to attack Marishka. "No, I've got her."

Melissa did her very best swagger to the black latex clad domme. "Marishka, Marishka, Marishka. What am I going to do with you? I have told you time and time again," shaking her head side to side, letting her hair flow around her, "that I am not your sub to order around. I have told you time and time again I am no one's submissive." Grabbing a hold of Marishka's tightly rolled French twist and yanking her to Melissa's level, she said in a very soft tone. "Get on your knees."

The tone, while soft, brokered no options. Marishka had enough submissive instinct to do what a domme demanded and slipped to her knees.

"Kiss Nick's shoes." Melissa commanded pointing at Nick; the brunette balked for a second but did what she was told.

"Melissa, no," Nick started to say to stop the humiliation of the woman, but Christophe caught his attention, shook his head, and then nodded once when she knee walked to the crowd.

"Now Marishka, before I find something less to your liking."

Marishka looked at the faces of the men and quickly leaned down and kissed Nick's shoe.

"I said shoes plural, not singular, kiss them both." Melissa saw the woman's shoulders slump, but do as she was told. "Now don't make me remind you again Marishka."

"Xavier's next." Taking a small pity on the woman who had bothered her for months, she added, "his combat boots."

Xavier understanding the need to give a torturer a little of their own back, stood still and watched the domme-gone-sub do what was demanded of her, even if she hated every second of it. He was sure he would never need to worry about his little sister again, well, this little sister anyway.

Looking at Sam's eyes to make sure he understood this was nothing against him, she said, "Now the pig's," Marishka's head jerked up and looked at Sam before it dropped again; she started to back up until she ran into Melissa's leg, "no, no, kiss Sam's shoes, Marishka." Melissa said harshly "Do it or you will find yourself on display."

"No, please."

"Then do it," Melissa ordered again, pushing her head down.

Nick squirmed and tried again not to stop this but it was so hard for him. He had never seen anyone treat another person like this. Why did Marishka take it and why was Melissa doing it. This had to be the same woman Christophe had been talking about earlier, but still, this was too much.

Finally giving in, Marishka kissed Sam's shoes and waited, "No." Melissa said, "Now you will go to the door and kiss the shoes of every man that comes in, and I'll know if you don't. You may rise but you had better not look at a woman the entire way and you will not touch a woman for the rest of the night. If I hear of you even breathing in a woman's direction you will be in the mirror room."

"Yes mistress."

Once the woman was gone, Nick grabbed Melissa's arm. "What the hell was that all about?"

"Control," Melissa said icily "she's been trying to control me since the first time I walked in here and I had finally had enough of it."

"You don't have the right to..."

"To what - tell the little dyke she can't touch a woman? Nick, you don't understand how it works here, you only have control over someone if they let you. She let me. I would never let her, so she wanted me more than anyone else. I stopped letting others control me the day I walked out of Aniello's house, I will never go back."

"I'm hurt my sweet." Christophe said.

"Oh Christophe, you knew I never let you control me I only..."

"Let me think I could make you do whatever I wanted."

"Usually what you wanted was what I wanted so it was no big," Melissa said smiling.

"Stupid question," Sam said, "why didn't you have her kiss his shoes?" pointing to Christophe.

"Because my dear, Marishka is already scared of him because of what he does. She's intimidated by male authority figures. That's why she was scared of you. You know I would never call you a pig, Sam, but I wanted to scare her before sending her off."

"Man, this is weird. What, wait, what if my sister...oh man, I have got to find her."

Melissa knew what Nickolas was thinking, someone was controlling his sister, and someone was making her do everything they wanted, whether she wanted to or not.

"Okay, Christophe, will you check The Hall and see if you can see her, or see if someone knows her?" Melissa pulled out the sketch and showed it to her friend.

"I have to get her cleaned up, I can't take this anymore. I don't want to keep worrying about her."

"We will see what we can do, Nickolas; come on lets go," Melissa said, "you two go into the bar and look around," pointing the way to Saver and Sam.

An hour later, the group was together again in the bar. Melissa had left for a few minutes to check on Marishka and found her exactly where she had been told to be. Returning to the bar, she stopped in the doorway and looked at the table that held her men. For a long time the only man she let close to her was Christophe. He had been so unlike Aniello, in both looks and demeanor. Aniello was very tall with salt and pepper hair and piercing green eyes. His voice had always been commanding and everyone scurried to do his bidding. Melissa had known she was bi-sexual when she lived there, and when she moved out here she had intentionally dated women for the first few years just because it would have never been tolerated at home. Then one day

Christophe caught her attention, looking so young and innocent even though he wasn't. Christophe was a study in contradictions strong and soft, kind and domineering at the same time.

Looking at Nickolas, Melissa had something happen she'd never in her life had happen before, her heart skipped. She had been pushing so hard to help Nick, she hadn't stopped to think why. Why did she care that this guy's hooker sister was MIA. Other than, no one should be missing and no one should be alone when trying to find someone they loved. Watching Nickolas speak to Xavier made her chest tighten. She shook her head but the feeling stayed. Nick leaned into hear something her brother of her heart said, and then Nick touched the man's arm. She was sure he had said something about one of his fallen brothers and her chest hurt again, seeing Sam pat Xavier on the back cemented her love even more. In less than a week she had fallen for a guy she didn't even know, just seeing him interact with her family seemed to be enough. She laughed to herself, needing to pull herself together before going back to the table, Melissa went to the bathroom.

She passed the common bathroom and went to one of the private baths in the back. She had a stash of make-up in one and she had gotten a little misty-eyed watching her boys. Along the way, she passed a scene room and stopped cold.

CHAPTER FOURTEEN

There on a table with the door wide open, tied to a table was Samantha. She was ball-gagged and was being fucked, while two men watched. The only thing wrong with this was the fact that Samantha was crying and that the men were counting a large stack of money. Melissa was fairly certain that the man wasn't hurting Samantha but it was obvious that she didn't want to be here. Trying to decide what to do, Melissa walked past as if nothing was wrong. She couldn't tell Nickolas that his sister was here, basically being raped, but she had to get her out of there.

Melissa walked quickly to the bathroom, touched her make up and walked back down the hallway. Stopping in the doorway Melissa said, "Hey, how much?" and raised her chin toward Samantha.

"She doesn't do girls," the twins said together.

"Well from the look on her face, I don't think she does boys either."

"We decide what she does," again speaking in unison.

"Hmm, how much for you to change your mind?"

"You can't afford it bitch, get lost."

"You might be surprised," Melissa was starting to get really pissed. These two were doing this shit in her club, it was wrong.

Samantha looked into Melissa's eyes as another stream of tears ran down her face. Melissa could see the scar Cassandra had added to her sketch. Christophe must have passed through here before they started because Cassandra had the drawing perfect.

"You want the bitch when he's done with her?"

"Yeah, or I wouldn't have asked now would I?"

"We watch," it was said as a statement.

"Oh, I don't think so."

"No deal," came in stereo again.

"What, you two perv's get off watching...can't get it up alone?"

"Bitch," spat one.

"Yeah, so, you say that like it's a bad thing."

"20k."

"Hmm, she better be damn good for 20k."

"She's not, but she's ours, so if you want her you pay our price."

"20k it is, you take plastic?"

"Ha, what do we look like?"

"Someone who doesn't take a check either."

"Fine, yeah, give me the number."

Melissa pulled her wallet out and tried to plan on how to get Samantha out of this room and out of the building alive. As sleaze one ran her card, sleaze two watched as sleaze three came. "So how do you want her?" asked sleaze two.

"Just the way she is, just without you three."

The man finally finished coming and walked away from Samantha, cleaned himself up, got dressed and left. Melissa made sure to memorize every detail of his face so she could tell Sam and get him the reward he deserved. The sleaze twins stood and walked out of the room.

"No leaving, the bitch stays here."

Melissa heard the door shut and lock from the outside, she knew this room and had used it once or twice herself. There was a camera in the picture to her back that could be watched from a room across the hall. Trying not to be obvious, Melissa leaned against the painting and said, "Samantha."

***

Samantha's head jerked, her eyes huge.

"I know you can't talk but I want you to listen. I know your brother and I have some friends here and we are going to get you out, ok?"

Samantha nodded.

"If I walk away from this painting they are going to be able to see us, so I'm going to act the part they think I paid for until my friends can get here? Ok?"

Again Samantha nodded.

Walking over to Samantha, Melissa ran her hand over her arm and up to her breast; she leaned over and kissed it, "I'm sorry if this is not what you like," taking the gag out of Samantha's mouth.

"It's okay." Samantha said hoarsely, "I...I... do you really know him?"

Melissa leaned into Samantha's ear, "yes, Janie, I really know Nickolas. He's been looking for you. I have a panic button in my pocket. I don't want to use it right away, I want them to think it's all good before Xavier and Sam come, okay."

"Okay."

"Let me get you a glass of water," Melissa walked to the sink trailing her hand down Samantha's leg. "We should clean you up a bit too before your brother comes."

Samantha tried hard not to react to the mention of her brother, "He's here?" she whispered.

"Yes, we came looking for you. Drink," Melissa said helping the girl sit up. After taking a few sips, Samantha shook her head when more was offered. "Come on, let's get you untied," she said, carefully undoing the ropes so that they didn't irritate the burns more.

"Can you stand?"

"Maybe."

"Let's see," helping the girl off the half table, Samantha dipped for a second but held her own. "Okay, there's a bathroom right here," opening the door, Melissa sat her down on a chair and got a washcloth out of the cabinet. She washed the streaks of salt away. Pulling her hand up, Melissa bathed the rope burns with a cool rag. "Do you want to?" nodding to the toilet.

"Yeah."

"'K, I'm going to turn around, 'cause if I go out they'll wonder."

"Okay, why are you helping me?"

"Because I like your brother, he needs to know your safe. You know he doesn't judge you, but he does worry."

"I know," Samantha whispered. "I, I've been so lost since our parents died."

"Honey, that was years ago, you need to get cleaned up."

Just above a whisper Samantha said, "I don't know how to be clean anymore."

"You are going to have to learn, but I'm betting you're working on it now."

"I'll try."

"Samantha, you have to do more than try."

"I'm done."

"Do you have any clothes here?"

"No, they burned those weeks ago when we ended up here."

"You're sleeping here?" Melissa asked.

"Yeah, they lock me in one of the cellar rooms."

"Hmmm, there are going to have to be some changes made."

"What?"

"Nothing," Melissa sighed pulling a robe out of the closet. It was short but better than leaving Samantha naked, it did nothing to cover the bruises on her legs or the scratch marks.

"You ready?"

"Yes," Samantha said shakily.

"Okay," Melissa opened the door to the main room and found it still empty. She had been slightly worried; pushing the little button, Melissa told Samantha "My friend said it can find me within three feet."

Samantha nodded, "How long do you think it will take?"

"Not long but just in case, come here."

"Can't you call him?"

"Left my cell on the table where he's sitting."

"Oh." Samantha walked over to Melissa, "He was right, I've never been with a girl."

"It's okay, we'll just play. Lie down on your stomach."

"Um, oh, okay."

Melissa pulled out a cream from one of the drawers that would help the bruises fade faster, counting in her head how long it had been since she called for Xavier. Melissa rubbed the cream onto Samantha's skin. "How did you end up here Samantha?"

"I was dumb."

"Hmm, not to sound mean, but I got that."

"I, I needed a fix and Lasiter was gone. I..." Samantha sighed, "I went to the twins, and they decided I was too good to let go. They kept me so high the first few weeks that I don't even remember them. Then they started withholding unless I would ..." Samantha shivered and her breath hitched.

"I get it."

"The funny thing is, I haven't had anything in almost a week."

"Turn over Samantha."

Samantha swallowed and did as she was told.

"So you've been here for about a month."

"Yeah."

"The first couple of weeks I was still pretty high, but I remember some things. I was on the main stage once but they didn't like that anyone could watch, so then they moved me to these rooms."

"Hmm," then there was a knock on the door - a pounding really.

"You better not be in there, woman, I know you wouldn't submit to someone else."

"Christophe, ah, the love of my life." "No, Samantha, it's okay, he's my friend; it's a code we have."

"I don't even submit to you, bastard, now open the door."

Xavier opened it and looked between the two. "You're weird."

"We know," Melissa and Christophe said.

"There are two of them, twins. I'm sure they will be here any..."

"And what do you think you're doing with our merchandise?"

"Second." Melissa finished, "Yep, that would be sleaze and sleaze."

Nick rounded on the closest twin, "First, she's not your merchandise, she's my sister, second we are taking her home."

"No you're not, she owes us for the heroin she's shot up, figure she still owes us another 50k."

"Hmm, that include the twenty I already gave you?"

"Yep."

"We'll see. Now boys, you just landed yourselves in a little hot water."

"Oh really old man, how's that?"

Sam pulled out his badge in one hand and a pair of cuffs in the other, "You've just admitted to selling drugs in front of an officer of the law."

"Entrapment," sleaze two yelled.

"Nope, I didn't make you say you sold this poor girl drugs, I just heard you say it."

"Oh, and strike two, you said it in front of an officer of the court too, since I am also a lawyer," Christophe said pulling a set of cuffs from a nearby drawer. "I guess I'll have to put these on my room tab huh?"

Nick shoved his sleazy twin toward Christophe who was closer, and pulled Samantha into his arms. "Oh baby, are you okay, they have…" he couldn't begin to say the words to ask the questions.

"I'm sorry Nickolas, I'm so sorry." Samantha broke into tears and Nick picked her up "shush, hush, it's okay, I'm taking you home; shush, it's okay," became a mantra as he carried his sister out of the club and to his car.

Melissa looked at sleaze a and b, and said "Sam, you haven't read them rights or anything yet, right, so they're not in police custody or anything yet, right?"

"Not technically, I need to call it in."

"So go use the house phone and call it in."

"I'll go with Sam," Christophe said, walking the man away.

"So what are we doing that Sam and Christophe can't be here to see?"

"Oh nothing much, nothing much," Melissa walked to the closest twin and side kicked him in the knee. When he went down she stepped on his throat. "You know what's really cool about these particular boots Xavier?"

"No, what's that?"

"They have this perfect arch for keeping someone pinned but able to breathe, well mostly able to breathe."

"I'm afraid to ask how you know this."

"Yeah, you should be."

Sleaze two started to lunge for Melissa, but Xavier caught him by the hair. "Oh man, his pony tail is slimy," grabbing the back of the man's shirt, he wiped his hand off down the back of it.

"Thought so, they ooze slime. This one is almost blue, I suppose I should let him up." Stepping back, Melissa let the dealer up. "Hmm I wonder," she said reaching out and grabbing the man by the balls. "Yep that's what I thought, no balls at all, and only a limp dick too." Gripping hard she shoved him into the metal chair he had been sitting in earlier. "So I wonder if I can let a few old friends know what you guys like and see if they can have you tutored in a new style."

"Melissa, you wouldn't?"

"Wouldn't what? Let a few lifers know about some fresh meat who think it's okay to use a woman that way? I mean come on; I'm all for a little humiliation and a good show, but really, these guys," Melissa said pushing the other twin into a chair and putting the spiked heel of her boot in a precarious place, "are too much. Janie didn't want to be here, she didn't want to be doing this," with a wave of her hand, "for them. She wanted to choose who she let into her body, she wanted to have the option to say no, that's alright, I'll pass," rocking her boot back and forth so that it slid father and father into the twin's crotch.

"I'm slightly surprised, Melissa."

"What?"

"That you know lifers."

"You don't know half of my secrets, Saver. It's just struck me these two haven't talked since Sam left. You think we scared them mute?"

"Naw, think they're just smarter than they look and don't want to fess up to some other crime. Oh hey, like kidnapping, since they did take Janie against her will, and pandering, I'm sure there will be other charges."

"Yeah, I can add one, trespassing."

"How do you figure that one?" Sam said coming back into the room looking at and ignoring the placement of Melissa's boot.

"Oh, well see, there is something you guys will learn quickly enough."

" 'K…" Saver drawled out, all three men waiting to hear her confession.

"I sort of, well kind of…" Melissa sighed, "I am a part owner in this club."

"Sort of, kind of?" Xavier asked.

"Melissa, you realize that with your permission I didn't need a warrant and this would have been a hell of a lot easier."

"No one knows, Sam, I'm a silent owner. This is one of the places my dad owned, I inherited my share."

"Your dad's dead?" Christophe asked.

"Look, deal with these icks," Melissa said, grinding her heel in and making ick one cry out and the other four men cringe in sympathy, "and we'll talk about the rest.

Let's take them out the back so no one sees them, I don't want to cause problems."

CHAPTER FIFTEEN

A couple of weeks had passed and Melissa had only gotten to talk to Nick once on the phone. She found out that he had gotten Samantha into a rehab that was more home than facility. They had a therapist there who had once been a prostitute and a drug user, so she would understand better what Samantha had gone through.

It had been decided to treat Samantha and Janie more like a case of split personality than one person; treating both her addiction and need to use sex to escape, differently than her depression and sense of abandonment at the loss of her parent's years ago.

Nick had been visiting daily, and between taking extra call center shifts and sleeping, it left little time for anything else.

Xavier and Sam had called a few times to ask her about this or that about the club, but nothing to do with what had happened the night they rescued Samantha.

Maybe it was all in her head but her family seemed to be avoiding her. Cassandra had been spending more time at the ranch; Yvette was talking to everyone under the sun about the move. Emiko was with her grandmother and Yukio, her grandmother's boyfriend. Anne was helping Robert more at the bar, and Melissa was alone. Even Aniello had been calling less. With everything that had happened at MINE! she had almost relented and answered once, but stopped herself before she did. Even Jasper and Tiny hadn't been there when she stopped at Sundry the night before.

Feeling lost, Melissa tried to forget about her problems, using the internet, but everything she tried only ended up reminding her why she was there. She shoved away from her desk when a pop up made it through her blocker with an ad for family game night from one of the board game companies.

Deciding it was time for something to give, Melissa grabbed her coat and drove to Michael's. Pulling up in front of his shop, she stopped and turned to look down the sidewalk. About four stores down was half the sleaze twins. She had never bothered to learn their real names, instead sticking with what fit. The ass had the balls to smile, wave and walk away. Melissa growled and walked into Michael's.

"My love, what are we doing today?" Michael said, pulling her into a hug and kisses.

"Something different," she shrugged, "dealer's choice."

"Really," he replied eyes wide. "Well then, I think you are going to have to have a facial too."

"Why would I do that?" Melissa asked hesitantly.

"Because then you will be too mellow to drive me nuts asking what I'm doing." The couple laughed and walked to the back of the shop. Michael called one of the other girls up and she started working on Melissa while Michael debated on how to best change Melissa.

Three hours later Melissa was mellow, but it didn't last long when Michael held the mirror up for her to see. "What the hell did you do?! Damn it - this is, this...its... damn it, Michael!" Melissa was completely in shock at the blond locks that moved when she moved. "Michael, I hate blond, you know that."

"You said different."

"Not crazy!"

"Baby, most people would call midnight blue crazy," Michael pointed out, hand on his hips. "You are gorgeous as a blond."

"So I'm chopped liver with anything else?"

"Oh, you are in a mood. You are gorgeous any color, but as a blond you are.." Michael put both hands over his heart and patted it, then pretended to swoon.

"Drama queen."

"Nope, I leave the drama to everyone else."

"I hate you." Melissa said signing the credit receipt.

Outside she looked up the street but saw neither twin. Feeling a little better, she drove to Saver's office. Pulling up, she saw Sam's beat up Jimmy.

"Hey guys, were you going to tell me that thing 1 and thing 2 were out on bail?"

"I just found out, Melissa," Sam said. "They posted this morning and the captain called me about fifteen minutes ago."

"Did you call Nick and Samantha?"

"Yeah, Nick is on his way to let the rehab supervisor know."

"Ok."

"So, blond?"

"Shut up if you want to keep breathing, Xavier."

The marine laughed and picked up the ringing phone, "Save Them For Me."

"Nick. Calm down. Nick, whoa, hey, slow down, Nick. NICK, BREATH. Okay, Sam and I are on our way."

"They got Samantha. They beat three other patients and one of the staff and drug her out of her room."

"Oh shit."

"He said they left a note saying she's theirs, and if we come to get her again we'll get her back in pieces."

"Oh how cliché." Melissa muttered.

"Cliché or not, I don't think they're playing around. Lock up for me, Melissa," Xavier called over his shoulder as he ran out the door.

Standing in the middle of the empty office, Melissa's head spun. Why would they want her so badly? Samantha may have owed them quite a bit of money for the drugs she had used, but truthfully, most of it had to have been drugs they had forced on her, there was something they were missing.

"Oh, for crying out loud," her phone rang again; she really was starting to hate that song.

"What, Aniello, why do you keep calling, isn't it obvious I don't want to talk to you?"

"Mio bello, I need to talk to you though," came smoothly through the phone.

"Aniello, you said when I left I was done, you wouldn't call me."

"I know, bello, I know, but I have thought of many things since you left us."

"I can't be part of that anymore."

"I am not asking you to be."

Melissa stopped, pulled the phone from her ear, looked at it, shook her head once, "You want to repeat that? I think the line got messed up somehow."

"It did not, il mio Tesoro."

"Don't you 'my darling' me, what is going on?"

"Melissa, I do not wish to have this conversation with you on the phone. May we meet?"

Melissa heard the tinge of fear in Aniello's voice.

"Please, bello."

In all the years growing up, she had never heard Aniello say please, not once. "Fine, I'll meet you at the airport."

"That won't be necessary, bello."

"If you tell me you're already in town, I'm going to be very angry, zio."

"No, I am not in town but I am only a few hours away."

"You drove here not knowing if I would see you?"

"I hoped when I got there you would take pity on an old man and see him."

"Ha, you are not an old man."

"Well, not so much, but it was worth a go, eh?"

"Fine, call me when you get to town. I'll let you know where I am. There are some problems with a friend that I need to see if I can help with."

"May I be of help, mio bello?"

"Maybe, actually yeah, maybe. I need to talk to them first. Aniello, I have built a good life here, they really don't know about my past, and I think I like it, but if them finding out helps Samantha then they find out."

"Il mio Tesoro, if they are as good friends as you deserve, they will understand and accept you."

"Maybe. Look, I better go, it's going to be hard tracking everyone down right now."

"Arrivederci."

CHAPTER SIXTEEN

Melissa drove to Magical Ways to see Yvette and let her boss know what was going on. Yvette had a soft spot for Samantha and Nickolas both. She had promised Samantha a week's worth of outfits if she stayed clean and found a job.

"Yvette, Yvette!" Melissa rushed in the back and started yelling but ran straight into Anne.

"Melissa, who lit your boots on fire?"

"The sleaze twins!"

"What?"

Stopping to take a breath, Melissa said, "The jerks that had Samantha, took her from the rehab house and left a note saying if we tried to get her back, she would come back in pieces!"

"Could they get more..."

"Don't, I already did that one."

"Damn it, why did you..."

"'Cause I was there when Saver found out."

"What did he find out?" Yvette said coming around the corner with several scarf boxes in her arms.

"The Brothers Grimy have Samantha again and did the cliché thing of saying if we tried to get her back..."

"It would be in pieces," Yvette surmised.

"Yeah," Melissa said flopping into a chair. "I should have just smashed their heads in when I had the chance. It was my club, I could have come up with some good reason."

"Melissa, you know you..."

"I know, I couldn't live with myself, yadda yadda, but I am the one who has to live with the look on her face when I found her."

Anne hugged her little Goth and soothed her hair. "I like the blond, by the way, it looks good, but that's for another time. What are we going to do?"

Melissa scrunched up her face and said, "I, uh, I may have reinforcements coming."

Yvette raised an eyebrow and waited. Melissa squirmed in the chair but instead of answering the unasked question, she pulled her cell from her pocket and made a call.

"Hey, you with Sam and Nick? Good, come to the shop, I've got an idea. Yeah, the back. Thanks Xavier."

Closing her phone she asked, "Where are Cassandra and Emiko?"

"Emiko's on the floor and Cassandra will be here in about twenty minutes."

"Why?" Anne asked.

"I'll tell everyone when they get here."

"Melissa, what is going on?"

"No, not till everyone's here. Wait, call Cassandra, and have her go back and get James, I need everyone."

Thirty minutes later the store was closed and everyone was in the stock room, waiting for Melissa to tell them what was going on.

Melissa kept pacing and whenever she got close to Cassandra, the empathic witch would flinch. Melissa would mumble, "Sorry," and pace again.

"Melissa, cheri, what is going on? You wanted us all here, now we're here, and you're not talking, mon peu l'un." (my little one).

"I know, I just," Melissa stopped and turned to the group, "I just love all of you and don't want to lose you guys."

"Melissa, we aren't going anywhere, we love you too." Anne said.

"I should have made you call Robert, he should be here."

"Darling, he's asleep. I can tell him what happens later, he's been pulling doubles."

"Why... no answer later, I have to say this."

"Say what?" James asked.

"My godfather is coming to town," There were a few small gasps but mostly there where blank stares, "Aniello is, well, should be here any time, and I asked him to help us get Samantha back. These slimes seem to think that they are mob like, so I thought I would introduce them to a real mob boss. One who has been the don for many years and who got that way at a very young age."

The room was silent, no one even breathed, and then James laughed, "You really are a mob boss's goddaughter!"

"Yeah, he's more of an uncle thought," that only made James laugh harder.

"Please excuse him, he's temporarily insane. Heat stroke," Cassandra said, smacking James on the back of the head.

Josh shrugged his shoulders and Alex shook his head. The pair hadn't known James long yet but they had gotten use to his sense   of humor.

"Oh sorry, woooh, the first day I met Cassandra, she said that your father worked for the mob, and that his boss took you in when he died, and I said something about you being like a niece, so it just was funny. Sorry, bad time for humor but…"

Nickolas spoke up, "It's okay, I don't care if he's head of the whole Italian mafia as long as he can get my sister back."

"No, he's not that big. Sam, you can't, I mean, I..." Melissa's shoulders fell. She had just outed her godfather to a cop; that wasn't going to be good.

"Huh, what did you say? I fell asleep, your uncle's coming to visit. I'm glad you two are reconciling." Sam said, pretending to stretch out kinks from his imaginary nap.

"Shouldn't you have called Christophe to come too though?" Nick asked, confused suddenly.

"Why?"

"Isn't he your boyfriend?"

Melissa laughed, "Oh god no. We, hell, I don't know what to call us. Bff's with benefits? Fuck buddies who are bff's, I don't know. I'm not what he's looking for in a partner and he's not what I'm looking for."

"You two aren't..?"

"No, Nick, we're not. Is that what you thought?"

"I didn't know what to think truthfully."

Melissa started to say something but didn't want to air any more of her laundry, clean or dirty in front of her family. "We'll be right back," she said to everyone as she grabbed Nickolas's arm and pulled him into the office, closing the door.

"Mon peu l'un is growing up."

"English, Yvette, some of us don't speak Creole."

"Some of you don't speak French either, mon garcon," she said to Xavier looking a bit taller.

Xavier shuddered and said, "Yvette, you know every time you do that thing I want to cringe."

"What thing, pettie?" Yvette asked with a wicked smile.

***

As the group distracted themselves from their worry for a friend, and their curiosity, Melissa was kissing Nick into next week.

When they pulled apart to breathe, Nick said breathlessly, "What was that?"

"A kiss."

"That was not a kiss, that was a, ah, oh hell, I don't know what it was."

"A kiss," Melissa said again, "I've wanted to do that for week, but I knew you had other things to worry about."

"Well, I was worried about you; I just didn't think I had the right."

"Nick, why did you think I was with Christophe? I mean we did sleep together, and for most people that means exclusivity, but..."

"Melissa, I'm not dumb. I understand, well sort of understand, the lifestyle you've been living in. Besides, the day at Denny's you smelled like cologne, then the other night when he came up to you like that and kissed you, I smelled it again. And then the whole thing outside Samantha's door."

"That was something we came up with a few years ago when some sub he was with once wouldn't leave him alone, but we knew Mary had backed off another dom when she found out he was married."

"Ah, uh, ok."

"I know we're weird. I don't *have* to live that way. I..."

"Melissa, lets figure it out as we go. I could learn to like it or not, we'll figure it out."

"We should go back out there before they think I'm fucking you blind in here." Pulling the door open, Anne fell on her foot and Cassandra caught herself on the doorjamb before falling on top of Anne.

"I knew you weren't fucking him blind, you were too quiet," Christophe said leaning against the wall across from the office door.

"Christophe, when, how, why.." Sighing and giving up, Melissa merely said, "Hello Christophe."

"Hello, my love," kissing her on the cheek and as he pulled Nickolas into a hug, he whispered into his ear, "She is very important to me. If you hurt her, there won't be anything left for the rest of these guys to pick their teeth with, got it?"

Nick leaned back so he could see Christophe's face, he looked nothing like the boy he had seen that first time in the bar. "Got it, man."

"Good," and then the boy was back, "so do I get to meet the godfather too?"

And as if speaking of him had called the devil, the devil called back. Melissa shook her head and answered, "Where are you? Why does that not surprise me, zio Aniello?

Fine, come around back, I hope you didn't break any speed limits getting here," walking to the back, she propped open the door, "The answer is yes, Christophe, because he's here."

Everyone shifted toward the open door and waited. A moment later an Escalade pulled up followed by a limo and another Escalade.

"For Christ sake," Melissa said. Then she yelled out the door, "You didn't tell me you brought everyone, Scopa Aniello merda." Melissa stalked back to the front of the room and dropped into a chair. "I should have known. Why did I think it would be just him and Tony? 'Cause I'm stupid." Melissa watched her family parted as her family filed in.

"Mel, you haven't changed a bit."

"Ah, look at little Mel."

"Ah, the bambina, she all grown up."

"Boys, boys, the bambina is about avere il cazzo in aria. Maybe we should say hello first." The mob of men stopped and waited for a man in his sixties with salt and pepper hair to walk over to Melissa.

Melissa stood and poked a finger in his chest, "Aniello, if you 'Mel' me even once, I will knock you out. She's gone."

Aniello bowed gracefully once and said, "No 'Mel' it is then, mio bello."

"I am not your beauty either, damn it, just plain old Melissa."

"You have never been plain, my dear, and you are not old."

"Oh shut up."

She took a breath and finally looked around fully. Her old family was on one half of the room, her new family on the other half. She looked for Saver and found him with his back all the way to the wall and breathing heavily. "Send the boys out," Melissa said whirling around and stepping up into Aniello's face.

"Pardon?"

"Send them out now," she growled through clenched teeth, she couldn't let them see Saver have a flashback, she wouldn't do that to him.

"Partirci," all the men turned to leave, a few of them with looks over their shoulders at Melissa but none stayed behind.

"Aniello, no more Italian, English only."

"Mio."

"I mean it, damn it, this is my family and my place, I make the rules here."

Aniello bowed again, "As you wish."

Quickly glancing at Saver, Melissa saw he looked less stressed and had taken a step from the wall. He caught her eye and before he looked away he nodded once. She nodded back.

"Aniello, this is my family, my brothers and sisters and a new uncle."

"Ladies and gentlemen, thank you for taking care of mi... my heart for me," turning to melissa Aniello said, "We have missed you."

"Yeah, well, look, I want to talk but I think we should get to figuring out how to get Samantha back all in one piece."

"Is this the friend you spoke of earlier?"

"Yes, she is Nickolas's sister," pulling Nick toward her.

"And who has her?"

Melissa looked to Nick and waited, he shrugged and she started the story "Samantha is a heroin addict and a prostitute. She went missing about two months ago. Nick looked for her alone for a month or so before he met me. Xavier is starting a private investigation firm so I told Nick to talk to him. Sam is an old friend of Xavier's who is also a police officer. So they were able to track down who she got her drugs from, but that changed awhile ago because that guy got caught. Two new guys took over and for some reason decided they were going to take Samantha over. A couple of weeks or so ago we found her at..." Melissa paused for a moment; she knew Aniello would recognize the club's name as soon as she said it. "We found her at MINE!"

Looking down at Melissa, Aniello lifted one eyebrow and said one word, "MINE!"

"Yeah, MINE!"

"Why is MINE! such a big deal?" James asked.

Aniello opened his mouth to say something, but didn't when Melissa hit him in the arm.

"MINE! is a fetish club my father used to own. When he died, it went into a trust until I turned 21. It's run by a very competent businessman, but I own it. I..." taking a deep breath and squaring her shoulders, Melissa decided no more secrets and continued, "I also go there as a member a couple times a month."

"Melissa, we know that you are a bit different, we don't care. We may not want full details but we only care that you're safe and happy," Cassandra said.

"I, on the other hand, am a little taken aback, but I have not seen you in eight years. But this is something else we can talk about later. Do you think they are at MINE! again?"

"No, I had them barred; now I wish I hadn't. We can check just in case, but no, I don't think they will be there."

"So these dealers have your sister. How did they get her again?"

Nick looked at Aniello and said, "They broke into the rehab house she was at, hurt several people and took her. They left a note saying..."

"Let me guess, the old standby, come after her and you'll get her back in..."

"Pieces," everyone said at once.

"I was never that cliché."

"Was?" Anne asked.

"I am out of the business, but very few people know of it."

"Wait, what?" Melissa stuttered, "What?"

"I sold, traded, or turned legit what I could."

"Why?"

"Because, my darling, I have missed you," he said kissing her on the forehead, "and I knew I could never have you in my life again if I was still Don Aniello Russo."

"I, I, crap, that's why you have been calling me for months?"

"Yes; now how do we find these two?"

"They are twins, we have photos of them. I'll put out a bolo with orders not to approach."

"Hmm, give me a moment. What did you say their names were?"

"Slime one and two," Melissa said under her breath.

"Matt and Lyle Dawson," Christoph offered.

"Thank you, gentlemen, I'll be right back," walking toward the door, the godfather disappeared though it.

"So what do you think he's going to do?" Christophe asked Sam.

"Something I want to be at the station for when it happens, so I can honestly say I didn't know anything about it. Want to go talk about the Todd case at the station with me, review some of the things on the board? And maybe we should talk about Ford's handling of the case."

"Yes, I think I would like to talk about how IA should handle that."

The two left after saying their good-byes and Melissa said, "Thank god, now I don't have to worry about ruining their careers."

CHAPTER SEVENTEEN

As the group waited a few minutes, Nick walked over and took Melissa's hand in his. He looked at it, then at her, "This okay?"

"Mmhum," Melissa murmured. She was still nervous about her family knowing so much, but they were still here and they weren't yelling at her to get out. Now if the crew could take things in stride as well, maybe she could keep them all in her life, something she would have said no to twenty minuets ago.

She couldn't see Aniello throwing his crew over for her, no matter how much he missed her.

As if thinking of them had summoned them, all of the crew was back. Xavier was better prepared for the invasion this time and was able to keep from reacting.

"We know where they are, and we know where your sister is, Nickolas. Will you let us get her for you?" Aniello asked.

"Yes, just don't let them hurt her anymore, she's been through so much."

"We will take care of her; she is famiglia," one of the group said.

"Tony, I, thank you," Melissa said.

"It's okay, Melly," the big man said. He walked over to her and pulled her into a hug, "we have all missed our Melly, but we are back and she's not kicking our cans to the curb."

"Keep calling me Melly and I will. You could get away with that when I was eight but I'm twenty-six, I think I've out grown Melly."

"No, you will always be Melly to us."

"Who is 'us' by the way?" Yvette asked.

Aniello looked to Melissa and then started introducing his men. "Tony," pointing to the man who had yet to let go of Melissa, "is my driver. Junior is my bodyguard," pointing to a lithe dark skinned man whose height alone made him intimidating. "Sol is my," pausing for a moment, "business advisor." The man looked like a he belonged in a gym pounding a punching bag into dust as opposed to a sitting at a desk, "Vincent is my," another pause, "broker."

Yvette interrupted the man and said, "Mr. Russo, I think you can skip the renaming of their titles, we know what you guys used to do. I think we might prefer to know what they used to do for you, more than what they might be doing for you now."

"Hm, yes I suppose, Tony and Junior really are my driver and body guard, Sol was my money man, handling all of my accounts and knew everyone who owed me money and exactly how much. Vincent was a broker but it was in items, not stocks. Tommy, Mick and Mike as well as Sean, are my, well, hm, they are..."

"We're the ones that do everything else," Mick said in a think Irish accent.

Everyone looked at him, "Yeah, I know, *'what's the Mick doing with the Wops?'*, but hey, they pay better."

Melissa laughed, "You haven't changed at all, Micky."

"Nope, why would I, lassie, it's too much fun."

Nickolas chuckled lightly, "Well, this is interesting."

"What?" Melissa asked.

"The Italians and an Irish mafia are going to rescue a Russian mofia."

"I thought your last name was Todd," James said.

"It is, that was my father's name; my mother's was Natalia Morozov. Her family was in the lower echelons of the Russian mafia before the fall. And after; things got worse for them, so they left and made it to America. She met my father, changed her name to Becca, and married him. I found out when they died she had kept a diary when she was younger. It never said anything specific, just vague references about tattoos my grandfather had. I looked them up once and figured out the low-level part. I remember her saying how bad it was in Russia, after the fall of the USSR but she wouldn't talk about it."

"Well, let's go get the little kraut and get her home," Tony said, "I've been itching to do some good driving. This keeping it to 65 crap is for the birds."

"Tony," Aniello warned "only if need be, and there…"

"…Had better be a real need, I know, boss, I know."

All the boys filed out into the alley leaving Aniello behind. "You're not going?" Anne asked.

"No, my boys know how to handle things; if they need me then I haven't trained them well. Besides, they get rather upset when I'm in harm's way. They forget that I wipe the floor with their asses every other day," Aniello sighed and shook his head. "But if they get the job done and are happy than who am I to kill that joy. I have already killed most of their joy by going straight."

"They do not want to be," stopping and looking at Xavier, "white hats?" Emiko asked. He nodded and she smiled.

"Well, Tommy and Sean are okay with it. They are the newest, so they only worry about paying off mortgages and things like that. The others were a little harder to get to see the light, so to speak. Because they have been doing this since we were all kids, forty years is hard to go against."

Cassandra stepped forward, "You might want to watch Sol a little closer. I don't think he's as for this as you think he is. There is something there that is not right, not, well, something's just wrong."

"Hmmhum, yes, Sol and I have been going around about the numbers, and how much it has cost to go legal. Playing by the rules is costly. Bribes are expensive but so are taxes. He dislikes paying them."

"No, Mr. Russo, I mean he is more interested in having all of it. I could feel his anger and the hate building."

"I'm sorry, you could what?"

"Cassandra è lo zio di strega."

"Ah," the man watched Xavier, he had noticed the way the man reacted. "Melissa, can I talk to you for a moment?"

***

"Yeah, come on," Melissa said, going to the office again, "no eavesdropping this time guys, okay?"

She shut the door and waited.

"Your friend, the PI, he ok?"

"Saver has had a hard few years, zio, he lost friends in Afghanistan, and he had to watch. They were wiz's with languages. He's better, but we've kind of pushed him the last few weeks. He's not real good with large groups of people yet, and he was hitting the clubs with me, then with all the Italian, it's maybe stressing him a bit too much."

"Marine, si?"

"Yes, special forces recon. Don't mention it. It bothers him that he's not coping as well as he wants to. He's only been in therapy for a little while."

"Why did he not get help sooner?" Aniello asked, doing some quick math in his head.

"He tried, but he had to edit too much because his friends were lovers and their memories would have been tarnished; all the work they did would have been..."

"I understand, bello, your Nickolas looks like a good man though. I think your strega, Cassandra would be a better judge."

"She's an empath, she feels other people's emotions. I can only imagine what it was like in that room for her, the worry from Nick, the anger from Sol, the anxiety from Saver and me, as well as the sheer amount of curiosity from everyone else. Mick's humor was something she would have needed though."

"Hm, I don't..."

"Love and humor keep her strong, keep her from feeling the full strength of the emotions."

"So you, mio bello, are good for her because you are nothing but love and humor?"

"Ha, funny old man, anything else you want to ask before we go back out?"

"Hm, the big red head?" Aniello asked with a smile on his lips.

"No."

"What, I only wanted to know her name."

"It's Yvette and she's Cajun, she'll hex you, given half a second. You stay away from Emiko, as well as Anne. Well, Anne will charm you into the middle of next week, but Emiko is still scared of many things."

"Melissa, you know better than that, I would never hurt a fly."

"Naw, you just let Mike do it."

"Ah, well yes."

Re-joining the group, Melissa said, "So how long do you think it will be before the boys are back?"

"Hmmm, no hitches or glitches, the twins will be nicely detained for an undetermined amount of time in about..." checking his watch, "...20 minutes. And the others should be here with Samantha in roughly 45 minutes after that."

"Where are they going to be detained?" Saver said.

"Oh, we won't be seeing them again. I may be legit but I still have favors that are owed me. They will have a fine time getting back into the country when they land in their new homeland."

"Do we ask?" Anne questioned.

"No," Aniello replied, "we will leave it with the knowledge that they will not be treated well when my friend lets it be known what they were doing in their former lives."

"That's cryptic," Melissa said.

"As it was supposed to be. Is there a restaurant nearby that I could treat all of you to? I imagine the boys will be hungry when they get back."

"There are a few Italian restaurants nearby but nothing you would enjoy, I'm sure, Mr. Russo," Anne offered.

"Please, just Aniello, I have no wish to be so formal."

"Zio, you can't help it."

"Perhaps."

"What does Zio mean?" Xavier asked, "I, it's right there but I can't remember it."

"It means 'uncle', Saver. I'm sorry, I shouldn't use it."

"No, its okay, Melissa, you guys can't hide me from these things; I have to get past them. If I hadn't hid myself for three years maybe I would be better."

"But you wouldn't have been there that day for our Emiko," Yvette remarked.

"No, I wouldn't," The marine said, pulling his love closer to him.

"So, how about that food?" James questioned, "I'm starving, and there is no way we're making it back to the ranch in time to have Consuela feed us," James said wagging his thumb between him and the pair of men to his right.

CHAPTER EIGHTEEN

Roughly an hour and half-later, Tony came into the restaurant. "Nickolas your sister is at St. Lucas hospital."

Alex looked up at the name of Cecilia's hospital.

"Thank you, I need to go. I'm sure there is paper work and insurance forms and," Nick paused, taking a deep breath, "everything."

"It's been taken care of Nickolas," Aniello told him.

"What, wait, how would you know her insurance?"

"I don't, but I do have this nice little black card that says American Express on it. That card keeps questions from being asked in many places. And I can write it off on my taxes, if you don't mind that is?" Aniello amended.

"No, no, I no, it's fine. It would take me months to be able to pay the bill off."

"As I suspected. I have money to burn, so to speak, and maybe it should be going to help people."

"Thank you, Aniello, thank you."

"You can repay me by keeping this one happy," patting Melissa's hand.

"I will try. Someone give me a ride back to the shop, my car is there - never mind, I'll take a cab."

"Ha! You'll do no such thing ragazzo, I'll take you."

"Tony no, you stay here and eat. Keep Melissa busy for me; keep her here so I know where she is. Every time I try to find her she's somewhere else."

"When did you go looking for me?" she asked confused.

"Every time I walked into Sundry or any of the other Goth bars in this town, I would look for you, or, well, your hair."

"Hmm, this pretty blond hair in the middle of all that black," Aniello said as he slid a hand down Melissa's hair.

Nickolas laughed as he walked out the door with Tony following, he could hear everyone else laugh as well.

Alex caught up to them at the car, "I'll go with you," he offered.

Nickolas was getting use to offers of help from Melissa's friends, but still stunned him enough to ask "Why?"

Alex smiled, "My mom works there and I can help explain things to the staff and to you. I'm also a nurse."

Nickolas still had a headache from the first time Samantha had been checked into the hospital, and that had been mostly scrapes and bruises from being in the club for so long. He wasn't going to think about the mental part right now. It would be to much and he would end up shutting down and right now Samantha needed him. Nickolas shrugged, "Sure at least this time I'll understand what their telling me."

***

Aniello listened to his boys talk with Melissa's family. It pained him to think of them as separate groups but he would have to deal with it. He hoped that someday they would be one family for her, instead of this two.

Having lived life as he had, Aniello had to be a good judge of character and he had to be quick about it.

He watched the little groups that sat round the tables that had been pushed together to accommodate their large party.

Nickolas had returned from checking on his sister, who would be back in her rehab home tomorrow. Aniello would make sure there was an anonymous donation dropped off there, first thing in the morning.

Nickolas sat next to Melissa and this lawyer, Christophe. The two men were easing into a nice friendship. The way the three acted, Aniello could tell that Melissa had been with both men but neither was jealous of the other.

His attention fell to the strega and her cowboy. He was sure that Cassandra was right about Sol. The witch had spoken something he had feared would happen, but he would see what he could do about saving his friendship with his number one.

The couple was happy and laughing at a joke Mick had just told. James struck Aniello as a good man who would take care of his witch and treat her as she deserved.

Next to the strega was another cowboy, Josh. His partner, Alexander had left with Nickolas and Tony. Melissa had told the boys that he was a nurse and his mom worked at St. Lucian's. She explained that Josh was the cousin of Cassandra's dead fiancée and worked with James on the ranch. Alexander was with him when he heard about Samantha and they came in case Alex could do something to help, either as a nurse or if something from his grifter past would help.

The marine was very protective of his little Asian fiancée and her of him. She watched without watching for signs of stress on the man and she would hum the same song over each time it looked like the situation was becoming too much for him.

The cop, Sam, sat with his arm over the back of the chair the Marine sat in, Saver's, as they all called him, and he would keep the staff from getting to close or jarring the man. By now all of his crew had seen the scars on his shoulder and the few faint ones on the vet's neck. Aniello wondered how many more the young man carried both physically and emotionally.

Anne's Robert had come but still looked sleep worn. The bar he tended was short staffed and he was working double shifts to help. He watched the couple lean on each other and saw the sad smiles when his crew talked about their children. They were a happy couple, but one who longed to share their love with another person.

Aniello wondered briefly if his offer of sending Sean over to help at the bar would be accepted or not. Sean had often served at parties he had hosted over the years. He would ask Melissa later.

Yvette was the odd man out. The Cajun with the Bronx accent was the only one of Melissa's family not paired off. She was happy and content with that, but there still seemed to be an air of loneliness around the woman.

It had been mentioned earlier about calling the aunts, referring to Cassandra's triplet aunts, but decided that it could wait, and that they would call Marco's and take over the restaurant. Aniello had been surprised to hear that most of the group were orphans. Yvette, Xavier, James and Emiko being the only ones whose parents still lived, but little Emiko was not speaking to her parents, the reason was *not* being discussed.

The impromptu lunch was quickly winding down and the dinner crowd would soon come into the little Italian eatery they had unceremoniously taken over. The former mobster did a quick tally in his head and figured that leaving them a thousand dollar tip wouldn't be *too* over the top, not that he cared one way or the other.

He had noticed coming into town that there was no *Little Italy*, but there did seem to be a *Little Tokyo* where Emiko lived with Xavier, her grandmother and her grandmother's boyfriend. It also looked like there was a section that would be mostly French, though he hadn't really heard anyone call a place in a town *Little Paris*.

"What are you thinking so hard about, zio?"

"Nothing, bello, is your marine okay with this? We could have gone to this Marco's earlier."

"He's not my marine, but yeah, he's okay with it. So long as Sam and Emiko are close, he'll be fine. I think Cassandra is helping to."

"How, I thought you said she felt..."

"She feels, and when she needs to she can help other people feel calmer. I guess she could send other emotions too, but it's not her way."

Aniello only nodded in understanding, Cassandra had a great gift, and she used it well.

"So, what were you thinking?"

"I was just thinking that I hope your familieas can get along."

"I think if you can behave, it will be fine."

"I hope so, bello, I have missed you too much these last eight years. I am not sure I want to go on missing you."

***

Later that night after plans were made to meet at Marco's restaurant that weekend, Melissa was snuggled up to Nick.

Nick's fingers glided across Melissa's leg, "Sooooo, about this club of yours?"

Melissa stilled, "Yes?"

"What are the dues to be a member?"

"Free, remember I own it."

"Hm, but I don't."

"Saw something in there you liked, did you?"

"Yeah, you." Nickolas whispered before he kissed her. Pulling her up and on top of him, Nickolas slid into her and they both sighed. "I think I liked the jewelry you wore when you went too."

"Hmm, you liked that did you?" she said rising up then sliding back down his length. "I could wear it without going to the club."

"You could wear it anytime and anywhere, ahh, oh, oh… what was I saying?" Nick lost his train of thought when Melissa leaned over and bit his earlobe. "Oh yeah, anytime or anywhere you want."

"I bet," she said nibbling on his shoulder, "now, anything else you liked about the club?"

"Seeing you boss around other people was okay, but I don't want to share you."

"Don't want to share you either. Think we can figure out what will keep us both going later though."

"Oh yeah," Rolling over and pinning her, Nickolas nipped back at her shoulder as he drove her farther and farther over the edge.

When he felt her muscles clench, he let his own orgasm take him over and screamed, "Melissa!"

EPILOGUE

"How much is this going to hurt?" Nickolas asked with trepidation.

"We don't have to if you're not ready for this," Melissa smiled at him.

"No, just - just wanted to know what to expect."

Melissa explained, "The unknown is half the excitement."

"I, oh hell, go for it."

Melissa laughed when the gun started and Nickolas jumped.

"It's only a silly tattoo, Nick, you'll live," Samantha chirped in.

"Easy for you to say," he mumbled but held still when the needles started to prick away at his skin.

"You'll do fine man, just go with it."

"Christophe, I'm going to deck you when I get done, this is all your fault."

"How? I'm not holding you in the chair."

"It was your idea, damn it."

A smile taking up his whole face, Christoph replied, "No, I just agreed that you should do it."

An hour later, after a lot of bitching and whining, Nickolas had his first, last and only tattoos.

On left side of his chest was a black scripted *M* with angle wings tipped in red. On the right side next to that, a pale blue *S* in the same style with slightly darker blue wings tipped with a brilliant blue.

Now both of his angels, his dark angel Melissa, and his light angel Samantha were forever near his heart.

ABOUT THE AUTHOR

Yasmina is from a small town in the middle of...naw you know better. Yasmina is originally from Vancouver, WA and then by way of the Navy and college ended up in Grays Harbor County with her husband and her two kids and now the two black cats. Yes, she has two of the furry beasts.

During the day, she keeps the people happy or tries to anyway. At night, she tries to keep her sanity by escaping aforementioned family to write down what the evil muses have shoved in her brain all day.

She waits for the graduation of her kids (one imminent and one not so imminent) so that the house will become quite.

She listens to an eclectic mix of music when she writes, anything from Shinedown to Nora Jones and a little of The Asteroids Galaxy Tour thrown in for the fun of it.

Her sarcastic sense of humor has and will continue to get her in trouble but hey who cares?

Yasmina has been writing between cries of MOM and YASMINA for ten years and plans to write for many more. Her first published stories were fanfiction for her favorite TV series but the first story she tried her hand at was Cassandra's Heart now available on Amazon.com, BarnesandNoble.com, Smashwords.com and soon in print.

Follow Yasmina on Twitter, Facebook, Shelfari, Linkedin, Blogger, Librarything, Wordpress and Goodreads.

Made in the USA
San Bernardino, CA
14 March 2014